W9-CIP-253

The Milly Stories

A MELANIE KROUPA BOOK

The Milly Stories

Corpses, Carnations, the Weirdness Index, and, of course, Aunt Gloria

by Janice Lindsay

A DK INK BOOK
DK Publishing, Inc.

A Melanie Kroupa Book

DK Publishing, Inc.
95 Madison Avenue
New York, New York 10016

Visit us on the World Wide Web at http://www.dk.com

Library of Congress Cataloging-in-Publication Data

Lindsay, Janice.
The Milly stories / by Janice Lindsay. — 1st ed.
p. cm.
"A Melanie Kroupa book."
Summary: Unlike her aunt, eleven-year-old Milly finds it very difficult to determine who's peculiar and who's not, even as she learns to understand and accept herself.
ISBN 0-7894-2491-6 (hc)
[1. Aunts—Fiction. 2. Self-acceptance—Fiction.] I. Title.
PZ7.L6599Mi 1998 97-36066
[Fic]—dc21 CIP
AC

Book design by Chris Hammill Paul.
The text of this book is set in 13 point Weiss.

Printed and bound in the USA.

First Edition, 1998

2 4 6 8 10 9 7 5 3

For Eleanor Campbell

and Glenda Baker

The Milly Stories

The Milly Stories

Good-bye, Aunt Gloria

"MILLY! Stand up straight! And stop fidgeting!"

Aunt Gloria had said those words to me a thousand times. I was startled to hear them now, though. I looked quickly at her in her casket. I half expected to see her inspecting me with raised eyebrows, the way she always had when she issued her "helpful advice." But she lay there as if she were in a deep sleep.

I glanced up at Uncle Edgar, then around the viewing room, to see if anyone else had heard the voice. The murmur of soft conversations continued. Maybe I was imagining things.

I slipped my hand into Uncle Edgar's big warm square one. He squeezed it gently and gave me a sad smile. We were already noticing how quiet the house was without Aunt Gloria's constant commentary to keep us company, and without the comfort of knowing that, for better or for worse, she was always there paying attention to us.

It was Uncle Edgar who was my favorite grown-up. I liked that he was tall and wide and unflappable. His balding head made it seem as if he moved through life more smoothly than other people.

Also, he didn't remind me at least once a week as Aunt Gloria used to: "Now that you're an orphan, Milly, you're lucky to have the two of us to look after you."

I knew I was lucky to have them, even though it took me a few months to get used to living in their funeral parlor. Uncle Edgar and Aunt Gloria had lots of overnight guests, but not the kind most people have. Their guests never ate or talked or partied, and each one spent the night in the embalming room or the viewing room, where Aunt Gloria was lying right now.

I liked that Uncle Edgar had stuck up for me when I turned eleven and Aunt Gloria made me put all my dolls in the attic. She had said firmly, "You play with those dolls too much. It's time you learned to grow up and act like the young lady that I know you are inside." Aunt Gloria said everything firmly.

Uncle Edgar hadn't been so sure. "What's the hurry?" he had asked in his soft, deep voice. But the dolls were all up there, packed in two big cartons.

I was wishing I had my dolls to talk to tonight. At least I'd know what to say to them.

I did *not* know what to say to all the people crowding around me now.

It seemed that everybody in Bentwood was at our

house saying good-bye to Aunt Gloria. People I didn't even know were hugging Uncle Edgar and me, holding our hands, patting us on the shoulder, saying they were sorry.

Then they'd stop at the casket to gaze at Aunt Gloria's round, pretty face.

"Doesn't she look good?" some people said in hushed tones.

I was glad they said that, for Uncle Edgar's sake. He and I had spent hours deciding which was Aunt Gloria's favorite dress so she would look just right to be buried. We smudged her lipsticks and rouge on the back of my hand to see which went best with the pink dress we chose.

Uncle Edgar had told me sorrowfully, "The heart attack was so sudden, and then she died. I never even had a chance to ask her how she would like her viewing. I want everything perfect—just the way she'd want it." I had watched him rearrange the floral tributes around her casket a dozen times trying to get them to look just right.

I was wearing one of those frilly "lovely" dresses that Aunt Gloria had made for me. The lace collar itched, and my hands kept bumping against the silly ruffles. But I wanted to look just right by Aunt Gloria's standards at least this one time, in honor of her viewing. My dress looked a lot like the one Aunt Gloria was wearing herself: She had made them both out of the same cloth. She said we'd both look good in that pink because we had the same "coloring," though her short curls were a much brighter blond than my long straight hair, which she had pronounced "mousy—ash blond, we'll call it."

Aunt Gloria had very particular standards. She told me once, "When you've been in town longer, you'll find that some of the people here are very peculiar." I didn't know how I was supposed to find that out, though. I wasn't allowed to spend much time with people she disapproved of, and she disapproved of practically everybody in Bentwood for one reason or another.

I did know a few people at the viewing.

Grandma, tall and thin and silver-haired, was striding around greeting people warmly. She always looked people right in the eye, kindly, as if she could see into their most secret hearts and liked them anyway. People smiled; they seemed glad to see her.

Once she bent over me and whispered sympathetically, "Hang in there, kiddo."

I remembered what Aunt Gloria had said to Uncle Edgar the day the article about Grandma appeared in the newspaper. The article was titled "Bentwood's Favorite Granny, the Preaching Biker." "Your mother's behavior is outrageous," Aunt Gloria had declared.

Flora, who ran the New Age Flower Shop, scurried into the viewing room, the skirt of her gauzy dress floating around her tiny ankles. Flora wasn't much taller than me and had a bushy tangle of bright red hair.

She crooned, "Milly dear, doesn't your Aunt Gloria look just like a beautiful angel, so peaceful and serene. I know it's hard for Edgar and you to lose her, but we must remember that now her spirit is free to explore all the far reaches of our glorious universe." Flora hugged me. Her tiny hands fluttered around me like the butterflies in her garden.

"An absolute flake," I heard Aunt Gloria say. I took another look at the casket. She was still dead.

The air in the viewing room smelled heavy and sweet from so many flowers. A fat lady wearing spicy perfume gushed about how pretty I looked. She gave me a bone-crunching hug. I couldn't breathe. I wished I could run up to my room, watch this silly frilly dress disappear like Cinderella's gown at midnight, and read a story.

"You read too much. Now stand up straight and be polite."

I raised my chin. Squared my shoulders. Straightened my back. Put my hands at my sides. Pressed my feet together. ("One, two, three, four, five, top to bottom," as Aunt Gloria had taught me.) I smiled as politely as I could at the fat lady.

I didn't know if Aunt Gloria could see me, or if I was imagining she could. But I had always figured that the least I could do for Aunt Gloria was to try to please her.

Anyway, no matter how much I wished to be out of here, I couldn't leave. Uncle Edgar needed me.

Charles Harkness, the stocky middle-aged banker who lived across the street, shook my hand lightly. He glanced at me, then quickly looked at the floor, mumbling, "I'm sorry for your loss."

"Ridiculously shy for a man his age."

Sandy-haired Angus MacDonald patted my arm sadly with his pale, bony fingers. "Poor wee lassie, to lose your dear auntie," he said, teary-eyed, in his Scottish accent.

"Weepy old fool."

I wished Aunt Gloria would stop interrupting, but it would be impolite to ask her to be quiet. It was *her* viewing, after all. Anyhow, what would people think if I suddenly started talking to a dead person?

Carol Jones, who was in my class at school, followed her parents into the viewing room. As always, the richest family in town looked as if they had just modeled at a fashion show.

Carol usually acted as if only rich and beautiful people existed, so at school she generally ignored me. She glanced uneasily at Aunt Gloria. Most kids our age wouldn't know what to do at a viewing, but apparently Carol had received some instructions on proper behavior, because she shook my hand dutifully and mumbled, "I'm sorry about your aunt."

Mrs. Jones cried, "Oh, you poor darling," and

hugged me against her designer dress, but not so close that the fabric might get wrinkled. Mr. Jones put his arm around me affectionately as if I were his best friend. "If there's ever anything I can do for you and your uncle, you'll let me know, won't you, dear?"

Their mushiness surprised me. I had never actually met Mr. or Mrs. Jones.

"Now, *that* family is just about perfect," I heard Aunt Gloria say. This did *not* surprise me.

My cousin Blane, sixteen and lanky, appeared at my side. He told me softly, "I hope you and Uncle Edgar are doing okay." For once he wasn't carrying his laptop computer.

"Likeable, but no common sense."

As Blane spoke with Uncle Edgar, I received more helpful advice. "Stop tugging on your collar. It's not that itchy."

I quickly lowered my hands. I thought, This house is going to be a lot more quiet for Uncle Edgar than for me.

After the viewing, Uncle Edgar stood at the door saying good-bye as people left. I studied Aunt Gloria's face. It didn't seem like her face at all. It had the same high forehead, the same arched eyebrows, the same sharp nose, the same thin pink lips. But it was too calm, too still. Aunt Gloria's face had never been this peaceful when she was living in it.

"Good-bye, Aunt Gloria," I whispered. "Wherever you are, I hope all the people there are perfect and polite and not too peculiar."

Driving the Brain Train

I SHOULD have known right away that my cousin Blane wouldn't make a very good ice cream man. At first I was too excited to think about it, though.

When Blane got his driver's license that spring, a few weeks after Aunt Gloria's funeral, Mr. Sauer at the Sweet Shoppe offered him a job driving the ice cream truck. Blane asked me if I'd like to take over his paper route. Me? A paper route! No more hurrying home right after school and staying there, as Aunt Gloria thought a proper girl my age should do!

I could hear Aunt Gloria: "What will people think, a young girl like you cavorting around the neighborhood?"

But I knew lots of kids who had jobs after school. I never knew anybody who cavorted.

When I asked Uncle Edgar if I could do the route, he just said, "Let me think about it."

Later I heard him on the phone with Grandma.

"Ma, I don't know anything about raising a girl. Gloria was the one who always knew what to do."

He listened. Then he said, "I know you do," and that's all I heard. But I figured Grandma said something like, "You'll do fine. I have absolute faith in your judgment." Grandma always had faith in everybody's judgment.

After a while Uncle Edgar told me I could do the route if I thought I could handle it.

I answered as calmly as I could, "I'm sure I can." I was trying to sound serious and responsible. But my insides were dancing like Ping-Pong balls in a breeze all peeping, "Yes! Yes! Yes!"

So one afternoon Blane showed me the route. He even gave me his bike, with a basket for the papers. I must have thanked him a bazillion times for the route and the bike. (He said I only thanked him twenty-two times.) The next afternoon Blane started driving the Goody Train. Because my paper route crisscrossed his ice cream route in lots of places, I saw with my own eyes how he got himself into trouble.

Blane would do any job to earn money for computer stuff.

He was totally logical and a certified genius—so the kids called him Brain, of course—but he wasn't smart. He could do complicated math problems in his head. He could improve a computer by taking it apart and putting it back together. But if he thought his English or history homework was boring or silly or just too easy, he wouldn't bother with it.

When the teacher asked him why he didn't do his homework, he wouldn't even bother to make up an excuse. He would just say in his good-natured way that it was boring or silly or too easy. His total honesty was always getting him into trouble.

All this was probably why Aunt Gloria thought Blane was a little peculiar: "No common sense."

The hot weather came early that summer, so we weren't even out of school yet when Blane started driving the ice cream truck with its loud, tinkly "Pop Goes the Weasel."

On the first day as I passed him, he leaned his tall, skinny body out the door.

"Hey, Milly! I'm going bananas!" he yelled. "I've heard 'Pop Goes the Weasel' three thousand five hundred sixty-two times!"

By the next day, he had hitched his laptop to the sound system and was playing not only "Pop Goes the Weasel" but tinkly versions of "The Waltz of the Sugar Plum Fairies" and the theme from *Star Wars* and Beethoven's "Moonlight Sonata" and some other stuff I figured he made up. None of the songs ever repeated.

That day, I happened to be delivering papers near a group of little kids waiting for the ice cream teenager. I stopped and waited, too. The first little girl asked Blane for a slush cone. Blane leaned over the counter as far as he could and motioned for the little girl to come closer.

"Don't buy a slush cone," he said quietly. "It's only ice chips with some sugar syrup. It's not worth the money. If I were you, I'd get an ice cream bar."

"Okay," she said happily, and bought an ice cream bar.

I could see that Blane was being his usual honest self, distributing advice as well as ice cream. This went okay as long as the advice revolved around selling ice cream.

But once I heard a boy ask Blane—actually, he asked "Brain"—how to find the square root of ninety-two. And of course my kind and helpful cousin told him, and didn't make the kid buy anything at all.

As I rode my route, I began to notice bunches of little kids holding notebooks and pencils. They were waiting for Brain. I realized that when Blane was doing the paper route, he must have been helping kids with their math problems or their science problems and maybe even their English and history problems, too. (He could usually figure out the answer even if he hadn't read the book.) Now he was doing the same thing from the ice cream truck.

One day I saw the Goody Train stopped in front of the Gates's house. There was Blane, standing on top of the truck, while Mrs. Gates's head was poking out her upstairs office window. She would yell something to Blane. He would yell something to her. Then her head would disappear. After a few seconds, her head would reappear and she'd yell to him; then he'd yell again, and she'd disappear again.

I could hear all the words, but I only recognized half of them. Since the only foreign language Blane spoke was Computerese, I figured that Mrs. Gates was having trouble with her computer.

I watched and listened for a while, trying to follow the conversation. Then I called up to Blane on the roof, "Why don't you just go in there so you can see what she's doing?"

"Can't leave the truck when I'm on duty."

"What if you had a pair of binoculars so you could see in the window?"

"Great idea! Do you happen to have a pair on you?"

"Of course not. Maybe you could ask Mrs. Gates if she has some."

So the next time her head poked out, he asked her. In English. No binoculars.

"I'll go to Gracie's," I offered. Bob and Gracie Arnold had just bought an old house around the corner. They were remodeling it to make a bookstore. I remembered, from visiting them with Aunt Gloria, that Gracie was a birdwatcher and kept a pair of binoculars on the kitchen windowsill.

So I sailed around to Gracie's as fast as I could. Aunt Gloria piped up with some of her helpful advice: "Slow down! You'll get yourself killed!"

I slowed down. A little.

I arrived at Gracie's kitchen just before I ran out of breath.

"Hello, Milly!" Gracie said, surprised.

"Hi. I can't explain right now, but may I please borrow your binoculars for a few minutes?"

"Sure. Is something wrong?"

"Nothing serious. It involves Blane and a computer."

"Makes perfect sense to me." She grinned.

Once Blane had the binoculars and Mrs. Gates turned the computer to the window, Blane, from his perch on top of the Goody Train, could see for himself what was going on. The whole process went much smoother when there was no head bobbing in and out the window. Blane promised to return the binoculars to Gracie, and I continued on my route.

I was doing my homework at the kitchen table that night when Blane slumped in.

Blane hardly ever slumped.

"What's the matter?"

"Mr. Sauer fired me today." He dropped into the chair across from me.

"How come?"

"He said I wasn't selling enough ice cream."

"And what did *you* say?" I was afraid he had said something honest but dumb.

"I said I've been helping kids with their homework and that's more important than selling them ice cream."

I was right. Honest but dumb. "It's probably not more important to a man who makes a living selling ice cream," I suggested.

We stared into space together.

I wished I could think of some way to help Blane get his job back.

Aunt Gloria put in her two cents' worth. "Don't stick your nose in where it doesn't belong, Milly. Mind your own business."

But Blane looked so sad. How could I just sit there and do nothing? It wasn't as if I had called him to ask whether or not he got fired today. He came to tell me about it all by himself. So maybe this *was* my business.

But what could *I* do? Argue with Mr. Sauer? Organize a boycott? Lead a march on the Sweet Shoppe? I'd be way too embarrassed to do anything so dramatic.

Aunt Gloria struck again. "Children should be seen and not heard." This time, I thought, maybe she has the right idea.

I asked Blane, "What do you think your customers will do when they find out you've been fired?"

"I don't know. Probably nothing."

"Let's find out."

The following day, all my newspaper customers received a note slipped into their afternoon papers. It was a computer printout, on orange paper so they'd be sure to see it. It said, "Blane George regretfully announces that, due to circumstances beyond his control, he will no longer be driving the Goody Train. He sincerely regrets any inconvenience this may cause his customers." The phone number of the Sweet Shoppe was in tiny print on the bottom.

Late that afternoon, as Blane told me afterward, the phone began to ring in Mr. Sauer's office. Just as I had hoped, unhappy customers were calling to register their complaints. Kids needed homework help. Grown-ups needed computer glitch counseling. They didn't care so much about the ice cream. People wanted their Brain back.

Blane phoned me that night, all excited. "I just talked with Mr. Sauer! We're going to compromise. I can keep helping people as long as I tell them they have to buy something. One ice cream for one problem. That should make everybody happy, don't you think? Thanks for your help, Milly."

Mr. Sauer painted out the name "Goody Train" and painted in "Brain Train."

Blane helped kids through the end of the school year. He helped kids going to summer school. He uncrashed computers. And of course he sold more ice cream than any ice cream person had ever sold before. He used his profits to buy software and enhancements for his computer and saved the rest for college.

My customers said I was as good a paperperson as my cousin (minus the homework help, of course). I got some big tips. I used the money to buy books and T-shirts and jeans.

And I had to admit that Aunt Gloria could sometimes be an inspiration.

Rancho Joyabounding

WHEN SCHOOL was out for the summer, Flora at the New Age Flower Shop invited me to sign up for her summer morning writing institute.

"You'll love Rancho Joyabounding," she said excitedly, patting my arm with her tiny hand and shaking her wild red hair. "We'll read a lot, and experiment with all kinds of writing. And a new girl in town will be joining us. She's just the nicest person. I'm sure you'll like her a lot."

Flora always thought everyone was the nicest person, so I wasn't counting on much. The writing might be fun, though. Some of Flora's poems and stories had been published in magazines, so I figured she must know about writing. And Blane helped Flora in the flower shop every morning before starting his afternoon Brain Train, so at least I'd have someone to talk to.

Uncle Edgar said yes right away. "No sense spending another summer in this old house all by yourself." It didn't seem to bother him that Aunt Gloria had thought "flaky" Flora was one of Bentwood's most peculiar people.

Rancho Joyabounding took place under the wide grapevine trellis in the garden behind the flower shop.

Here's who was there on the first day, waiting in a little circle of lawn chairs while Flora gave Blane some instructions inside.

There was Carol Jones, who everybody agreed was the most beautiful girl in town as well as the richest, and sometimes the grumpiest. She made it clear she was only there for something to do before she went to her real summer program, riding her very own horse, Blazing Champion, at the equestrian center. Carol talked a lot, mostly about herself and her horse.

Ashley, Carol's best friend, was there, too. Ashley was the second-richest girl in town. Whatever Carol did, Ashley did, except she didn't have her very own horse, so she talked about Carol's. As far as I knew, none of the other kids had ever seen Blazing Champion.

Right now, Carol and Ashley were discussing who in their crowd was having parties this summer, what all the girls would wear, and where to get your ears pierced. They grumbled that if only their parents hadn't made them come to this writing program, they would have a lot more time to think about these important matters.

Beyond saying hi, they didn't pay much attention to me. They never did. They had decided right after I moved to Bentwood that I was a bookworm and, more specifically, a bookworm without much money. So as they babbled on, I didn't feel bad about reading the short-story book I had brought along just in case.

Also at the writing institute were the Downey twins, Dmitri and Dimity, pale and thin and looking almost exactly alike. Everything about the world seemed to puzzle the twins. They were nice enough once you got to know them, but they were shy and talked mostly to each other. Most of the kids called them Dim and Dimmer, which they actually preferred to their real names.

Then there was the new girl. Nobody talked to her. She was about my height but not so skinny. Instead of having blue eyes and long stringy blondish hair, she had dark brown eyes and long stringy black hair. She looked at all of us and at the flowers and at Flora's big orange tiger cat stretched across the path while we waited to get started.

Finally, Flora burst through the door in her floaty, flowery dress, all five feet of her bristling with excitement and enthusiasm.

"Good morning, students," she practically sang. "Isn't this a glorious morning to be a writer!" Her fluttery hands swept to include us, the flowers, the leaves, the cat, the sunshine, the whole world, and probably the entire universe.

"I guess you all know each other, except for our new

friend Josie here." She patted Josie's shoulder affectionately. "This is Josie Martinez. She moved into Bentwood just last week. We're so happy to have you with us, Josie." Then she told Josie our names and Josie smiled and everybody said hi.

"At Rancho Joyabounding," rhapsodized Flora, "we will do lots of writing. But even more important, we will express our most beautiful thoughts. Find our hearts. Commune with our inner voices. Free our creative spirits. Open our minds to the universe . . ."

Aunt Gloria chimed in: "Flora's such an airhead, I'm surprised she hasn't floated away by now." I figured that when Flora said "commune with our inner voices," Aunt Gloria's was not exactly the type of voice she had in mind.

Flora went on and on; then, suddenly, she stopped. "Any questions?"

Dim and Dimmer looked at each other, too shy for questions. Carol and Ashley were rolling their eyes at each other, and I was just waiting to see what would happen.

But Josie wasn't shy. She spoke up, "Why do you call this Rancho Joyabounding?"

"I'm so happy you asked! At our summer writing program, we will have lots and lots of brilliant creative ideas. Every time someone has one, I want you to call out 'Joyabounding!' as an encouragement to everyone else. Can you all say 'Joyabounding'?"

"Joyabounding," we mumbled. Everybody else must have felt as silly as I did.

"Try it again, but with more enthusiasm."

"Joyabounding," we all said a little more loudly.

"I want you all to stand up and shout 'joyabounding' as loud as you can."

Josie stood up first, then I stood, then the twins. Carol and Ashley eye-rolled, but they got up, too.

"On the count of three," Flora said. "One . . . two . . . three . . ."

"*Joyabounding!*" we all yelled, so loud that Blane peeked out the window to see what was going on and the cat woke up long enough to glare at us. Flora looked pleased.

"Good," she said. "Now sit down. We can proceed. For our first exercises, we're going to awaken our senses to the world around us. Writers must always be aware of the sights, sounds, smells, tactile sensations, and even tastes that bombard us from all sides."

Flora played a tape of different sounds, and we had to guess what they were. Then she passed around a lot of small objects in plastic bags for us to feel but not look at, and we tried to identify them. Then she gave us plastic jars with different things for us to smell but not look at, and we wrote down what they smelled like. Considering that her collections included a scouring pad, yarn, cat hair, florists' clay, and glue, I was relieved when she said we wouldn't be doing tastes that day.

Finally, Flora said we were going to write something. "I want everyone to pick a partner."

Of course, Carol picked Ashley. Dim and Dimmer wouldn't dream of picking anyone but each other. That left me with Josie. Dim and Dimmer took their chairs to the far corner of the garden. Josie and I sat on opposite sides of the picnic table.

Flora said we should choose something we could see right now and write a glorious and vivid description of it. Then she stopped talking. Finally.

I could hear Carol and Ashley gabbing. By now, they were getting interested: They were going to write about how well the colors of their shirts and shorts blended with the colors of Flora's roses. The Downey twins were murmuring to each other, like always.

I couldn't think of anything to say, so I just looked around the garden for something to write about. Not that it mattered, because Josie spoke first.

"What's that cat's name?" she asked, gesturing at Flora's huge cat still stretched lazily across the tar path. In the patch of brilliant sunshine against the black background, he looked almost fluorescent, as if he had been dipped in a bucket of that orange paint that glows in the dark.

"Westwind Spirit."

"That sounds like something Flora would call a cat." Josie nodded.

Maybe all Flora's exercises to "awaken our senses" were starting to work, because suddenly Westwind Spirit began to remind me of something besides a cat.

At first, I couldn't figure out exactly what it was. But it was my turn to say something, and I blurted out, "In the sun, he looks like a speedbump."

"He really does!" Josie giggled.

She jumped up impulsively and headed for Westwind Spirit. "Come here, Speedbump," she said, and bent to scoop him up.

He struggled in her grasp, leaped away, and tore across the garden, disappearing through a hole in the back hedge.

"He doesn't like to be picked up," I said, too late.

"I noticed. Should we go after him?" she asked with a worried look. She checked to see Flora's reaction, but Flora had gone inside.

"Don't have to," I said. "Whenever he runs away, he runs to the same place."

"You're kidding. Where does he go?"

"To our house. We live around the corner. If he isn't back by the time class is over, I know the exact spot where he'll be."

"I don't believe you."

"Well, it's true. Anyhow, I think we should start writing," I said.

We both looked around the garden for a subject.

"I know!" said Josie enthusiastically. "Let's write about the trolls who live in those bushes, and how they come out at night to capture all the little garden toads and turn them into slaves for the Troll Queen."

"I don't think that's exactly what Flora would call a description," I said. This was going to be harder than I thought. "We're supposed to describe something we can see right now. I haven't seen too many trolls in the garden lately. Let's describe how the sun shining through the trellis makes those lacy designs on the grass."

"But how would we get any action into *that*?" Josie asked.

I suggested, "Maybe we could write about Speedbump." Except for Flora's exercises, he was the only subject we had in common. Even then, I wasn't sure what would happen.

"Okay."

I wrote the first sentence: "The orange cat stretched lazily across the sunny garden path."

Josie took the paper, read my sentence, and wrote the second sentence: "His tail twitched madly as he dreamed about dangerous adventures in the faraway cat kingdom of Althuria, where he had been a prince long ago."

As I was reading and thinking how far-out that was, Josie said cheerfully, "Joyabounding!"

She added, "Aren't we supposed to joyabound when we get a brilliant and creative idea?"

I wrote, "In the sun, Westwind Spirit was the color of the most radiant rose in the garden." I watched Josie read it. She raised her eyebrows. I said firmly, "Joyabounding."

Josie was not to be swayed from her course. She wrote: "Or maybe he was the color of the scarf he wore in Althuria, the scarf he gave the beautiful

Princess Ephesia just before he went into battle to win her hand." She smiled and said with loud satisfaction, "Double joyabounding."

I snatched the paper to my side of the table. I wrote, "Even the sounds of children yelling could not rouse him from his drowsy nap."

I said forcefully, "Joya-joyabounding" and passed her the paper.

Josie grabbed it. She wrote, "As he napped, he remembered the night he whispered to the princess, 'Call me Speedbump, for, although it may not seem like a romantic name, it signifies that I would lay down my life for you.' The End."

Then she raised both arms and shouted, "All the joyaboundings in the universe!"

Now everybody was watching us. Flora came out of the shop and said, "My goodness, there must be some truly brilliant and creative ideas happening out here in the garden!"

Josie and I looked at each other. She grinned. I was trying to glare at her.

But I had to smile in spite of myself.

Josie wrote a title at the top of the paper: "The Glorious and Vivid Speedbump in the Garden at Rancho Joyabounding."

We looked around. The others had started working again.

"I guess they're not doing too well," Josie whispered. "No joyaboundings."

Soon, Flora said it was time to stop working. We all

read our descriptions to the class. Josie read ours. Flora pronounced it "unusual for a description, but interesting." She said she didn't mind if we called her cat Speedbump because it certainly suited his personality, but she hoped he'd never practice in the road. Then the class was over.

Josie looked around the garden.

"Speedbump isn't back," she said. "Do you really know exactly where he is?"

"Yup. If you come home with me, I'll show you," I said.

Aunt Gloria jumped in: "Children running around a funeral parlor? It's just not appropriate." I had totally forgotten that Aunt Gloria never allowed me to have kids over. I'd never thought to ask Uncle Edgar how he felt about it. I was also totally forgetting what a lot of kids at school said about being in a house where dead people were overnight guests: It gave them the creeps. But it was too late to uninvite Josie.

As we walked, she told me she was taking this course because Flora had invited her, to help her meet some kids. Her parents had bought the farm supply store in town. She and her family had just moved to Massachusetts from New Jersey and she hardly knew anybody in Bentwood. She had four younger brothers and sisters.

Josie asked lots of questions. She wanted to know what it was like living in Bentwood. She asked me about Carol and Ashley and the Downey twins. She wanted to know about that cute teenager working in

Flora's shop. I knew Blane was a genius and a nice person. I didn't know he was "cute"!

After I had answered all her questions, Josie said, "I think Rancho Joyabounding is going to rate very high on the Weirdness Index."

"The Weirdness Index?"

"My brothers and sisters and I invented it. There's a scale of one to ten. Ten is the most weird. I haven't been to Rancho Joyabounding enough times to give it an exact rating. Don't you think Flora's a little weird?"

"That depends on what you mean by weird."

"Don't you think *this* is weird?" she said. She fluttered her hands, danced around on tiptoe, and searched the sky. "Today," she said in a high little voice, "we're going to commune with the universe."

I couldn't help laughing. "I suppose it *is* a little different. Aunt Gloria used to say Flora was flaky. But it was pretty nice of her to invite you to the workshop."

"I'll take niceness into consideration when I give her my Weirdness Index rating."

As we approached the Stone Church on the Corner, I pointed out my grandmother's house, the old one next to the church. Grandma was traveling, though—she was a contestant in a preaching contest at a church convention this week—so we didn't go in. Just as well. If Flora was scoring high on the Weirdness Index, I wondered where Josie would put my grandmother.

As we turned the corner in front of the church onto

my street, I stopped and waved enthusiastically like I always did.

"Wave, Josie."

"What on earth for?"

"Do it. I'll explain in a second."

"Are we waving at anything in particular?"

"That gray house, the fourth one on the left."

As we continued down the street I told her, "Two really old ladies live in that house. Hetty and Martha. They're sisters. Their nephew Charles bought a telescope for bird watching. But most of the time, when he's at work at the bank, they keep the telescope pointed at this corner so they can see who's going by. I always wave, just in case they're looking."

"I think I feel another Weirdness score coming on."

I was trying to act casual, but as we got closer to home, I was getting more and more uncomfortable. I was bringing someone without permission, and I hadn't warned Josie about the funeral parlor.

When I turned to start up the front walk to our house, Josie spotted the sign that said Edgar George Funeral Home. She came to a sudden stop.

"You mean you live in a funeral parlor?" she asked, wide-eyed. She hesitated for half a second, then followed me in. There was no viewing that day, so the viewing room was empty. Uncle Edgar was in the kitchen fixing lunch.

I introduced them. Uncle Edgar shook Josie's hand in both of his and said how happy he was to meet her and to have a visit from one of my friends. He even invited her to stay for lunch. I should have known he'd be so terrific.

"First I have to show her Westwind Spirit," I said.

We could have taken the stairs to the basement, but I thought Josie would find the elevator more interesting. She did. She stared at its long, thin shape and didn't say a word.

"It has to be this shape for the caskets," I explained.

When we reached the basement, I led her down the short corridor with its light gray walls and dark gray carpet.

On the left was the embalming room. Through the open door we could see the stainless steel embalming table, shelves of bottles, and shiny surgical tools on a white napkin on the corner table.

Josie peeked in. She whispered, with awe, "It looks like a hospital operating room."

"That's where Uncle Edgar gets bodies ready for viewing. It *is* sort of like an operating room."

On the right was the showroom. Six open caskets in different styles were displayed so that people could choose one. Inside, the caskets were like fluffy beds. Their polished outside surfaces gleamed silvery or shades of copper, bronze, or mahogany.

In one corner stood a special antique coffin that Uncle Edgar kept for decoration, a plain wooden box painted black. It was open.

I led Josie to it and pointed inside. There lay Speedbump, just where I knew he'd be, stretched to his full orange length. He lifted his head lazily, opened one eye, gave us his oh-it's-only-you look, and resumed his nap.

"See? I told you I knew exactly where he'd be."

Josie looked at Speedbump, then at me. "The Weirdness Index is working overtime today," she said.

Then she grinned. "I think I'm going to like living in Bentwood."

Call Me Cindy

JOSIE was busy nosing around my bedroom.

"Gee, do you think you have enough books?" she asked, gazing at the filled floor-to-ceiling bookshelves.

"There's no such thing as enough books."

This was the second time she had come home with me after a Rancho Joyabounding morning. The first time, she had asked Uncle Edgar a million questions about funerals and dead people, and we never got around to coming upstairs. Now we were there to work on a writing assignment.

"Is this your mother and father?" she asked, snatching the framed photo from my desk.

"That was taken the day they were married. Aunt Gloria gave it to me."

"You look like your mother. Do you have any pictures of her when she was our age?"

"My grandmother used to, but a pipe burst in her house a few years ago and the water ruined everything in the study, including the photo albums. I never even saw them. This is the only picture of my mother that I know of," I explained, carefully taking the wedding photo from Josie and replacing it on the desk.

"Don't you have any pictures from when you were little?"

"Dozens. But they're all of me. My mom was always on the other side of the camera."

"My dad takes lots of pictures of us, too. Mostly video. Do you miss your mom and dad?"

"I don't remember my father. He left when I was a baby. I think about my mom a lot. I guess it's because of her that I like books so much. She ran a bookstore in Los Angeles, and I used to read all the new kids' books. If I really liked them, she'd put a card inside with the 'Milly Moore Good Reading Seal of Approval.' She always told customers that was worth a hundred dollars. Not that they ever paid."

"When did you come to live in Bentwood?"

"A couple of years ago. After my mother died in the car accident, the family decided I should come and live with Uncle Edgar and Aunt Gloria."

"Was it hard getting used to living in a funeral parlor?"

"Sort of. It was harder getting used to living with Aunt Gloria. She was a little on the opinionated side."

I liked that Josie wasn't shy about asking anybody anything, but I was glad my closet door was shut.

She'd probably want to see all those frilly dresses Aunt Gloria had made in that "perfectly lovely" style.

"If you're through asking questions," I said, "maybe we should start writing."

"I know. I'm nosy." She shrugged cheerfully.

"Does anybody ever call you Nosy Josie?"

"Sooner or later, practically everybody."

Our assignment was to rewrite an old familiar story in our own way. Remembering our experience writing the Speedbump description, we decided to write separate stories.

But we both started with the same old familiar one. Here's my story.

"Call Me Cindy"

by Millicent Moore

Ella had to do all the sewing for her wicked stepmother and bratty stepsisters. So when they finally left for the king's fancy ball, she breathed a huge sigh of relief.

Just before they went out the door, Polly and Esther had recited their favorite poem: "Cinderella, Cinderella, you will never catch a fella." Then they held on to each other to keep from falling on the floor laughing.

"Finally," Ella said to herself as the door closed. "A nice quiet evening alone." She sat by the fire with chubby Fluffy purring on her lap and started to think up a poem.

Suddenly, she was startled by a bright light.

There on the hearth stood a tall, blond-haired lady, all in pink ruffles.

"Who are you?" Cinderella gasped. She jumped to her feet. Fluffy slid off her lap and scurried out the back door.

"I'm your fairy godmother," the lady said firmly. "I've come to get you ready for the ball."

"The ball? I'm not going to the ball. I'm going to stay home in the quiet and read some stories and write some poems."

"No, you're not. You read too much, anyway. It's time you learn to act like a young lady, get dressed up in something nice, and meet the right people."

"Would that mean I'd have to put on some silly frilly gown like the ones I made for Polly and Esther?"

"You can't go to a ball in that drab little dress."

"I guess I won't go, then."

But as Ella thought about the ball, she had to admit she was just a teeny bit curious. She had never been to a ball. But she had heard that they had very nice music.

"I know!" she said. "Maybe you could turn me into a mouse and I could go to watch and listen to the music!"

"Fairy godmothers don't turn people into animals. It's not proper."

Ella wondered what was the use of being

proper if it interfered with such a brilliant idea.

Fairy Godmother gave Ella a critical look. She raised her eyebrows. "You are a most peculiar person. Most girls your age would give anything to go to a ball. Do you want to go or not?"

"Oh, all right." Ella sighed.

Fairy Godmother waved her hands dramatically and chanted a few mysterious words: "Joyabunda, josiewunda, frillyunda." Suddenly, in place of her cotton dress, Ella was wearing a blue gown of the purest silk. It was way too fancy for Ella's taste, but she could see that she was not about to be consulted in matters of fashion design.

Instead of her worn-out shoes, she was wearing high-heeled glass slippers.

She hobbled to Polly's room to look in the mirror. Her hair, which usually looked like the top of a haystack, was now like spun gold. Some blue stuff around her eyes made them look big and shiny. Her freckles were gone. Her lips were pink.

"What have you done?" she cried in dismay. "I don't look anything like me!"

"That's the whole point. You look much better. And stop complaining. Someday you'll realize how lucky you are to have me to look after you. Let's go."

Suddenly the fairy godmother became a red-coated coachperson. She led Ella out the back door. A rotting pumpkin on the step became a beautiful coach, Fluffy turned into a white horse, and away they went.

As Ella got out of the coach at the ball, the fairy godmother coachperson ordered, "Watch the clock. At midnight, everything goes back the way it was. And remember to stand up straight and smile and be polite."

Ella walked into the ballroom, planning to find a dark corner near the orchestra where she could watch and listen. No such luck. Fairy Godmother had gone overboard and made her the most beautiful young woman in the kingdom. Everyone was staring at her. It was so embarrassing!

A host greeted her. He asked her name. She had to think fast. "Just call me Cindy."

Cindy was introduced to everyone, even her own stepfamily and, last, to the handsome young prince, who had been gawking at her along with everyone else.

Naturally, the prince asked her to dance. Somehow, when Fairy Godmother had made her beautiful, she had also made her know how to dance.

After a while, though, the dancing got boring. At last, the prince said, "I think I've had all the ball I can stand. Would you like to see the horses?"

"I'd love to!"

They slipped out and hurried to the stables. Cindy admired the prince's beautiful horses. She could still hear the music, and she and the prince got chatting and laughing and she realized she was having a wonderful time.

When she told the prince that she wrote poems, he said he did, too, and they made one up together.

The world is full of fancy balls.
We have to go, of course.
But if the choice were left to me,
I'd rather ride a horse.

They were working on a second verse when suddenly the clock began to strike. It was twelve!

"I have to go!" she said, running out the door.

"Wait! What's the hurry?" cried the prince.

Cindy ran for the coach. The fairy coach-godmother-person was waiting with the door open, pacing impatiently and looking at her watch. Cindy thought, I can't run fast enough in these silly shoes, so she stopped and took them off. Just as she jumped into the coach, she dropped one. There was no time to pick it up. The coach flew her home.

The very next day, the prince began searching for the girl whose foot belonged in the glass slipper. He visited every house, trying the slipper on every unmarried maiden.

As soon as the prince entered Ella's house and saw her standing by the fire with her haystack hair and her plain cotton dress and her freckles, he put the slipper in his pocket.

"I think I have found my princess," he said, gazing into her eyes. Then, much to the astonishment of Stepmother, Polly, and Esther, he began to recite a poem. "The world is full of fancy balls. We have to go, of course."

Ella smiled. "But if the choice were left to me, I'd rather ride a horse."

"Will you marry me?" he asked.

"I would like to marry you someday. But I have lots of things to do first."

"I'll wait for you forever. What shall I do for you in the meantime?"

Cinderella asked, "Could you please find a fancy castle for my stepmother? And some kind, rich husbands for Polly and Esther?"

So the prince did. And Cinderella lived happily for several years in her cozy house with Fluffy. The prince visited often. But most of the time, she worked on her poems.

Once, Fairy Godmother appeared, demanding, "Why don't you just get married?"

Ella replied, as politely as she could, "Dear Fairy Godmother, what's the hurry?"

Only when Ella was a famous poet, and all

the kingdom knew she was talented even if she wasn't as beautiful as they once thought, did she and the prince get married. They lived happily ever after. So did Stepmother, Polly, and Esther.

Ella never saw her bossy fairy godmother again. But she remembered to be just a teeny bit grateful. If it hadn't been for Fairy Godmother's interference, she might never have met the prince.

That was my story. In Josie's story, Cinderella was really a wicked witch who enchanted the prince so he would slay the dragon that lived in the woods near her house. The fairy godmother was a regular, kind fairy godmother (not crabby like the one in my story, Josie said), who pleaded with Cinderella to be a good person. But Cinderella wouldn't listen. Cinderella lived with three actresses whom she forced to pretend to be her stepmother and stepsisters so she would look like a normal innocent unmarried maiden. At the end of the story, Cinderella turned the actresses into toads. She turned the prince into a mushroom.

After I read Josie's story, I told her I knew she had come to Massachusetts from a place called New Jersey, but was that the New Jersey on Planet Earth, or was there another one?

She laughed. "Joyabounding," she said.

One Eight Hundred

WHEN SCHOOL started, our English teacher, Mr. French, didn't assign us to write "What I Did on My Summer Vacation." Instead, he told us to write "Something That Might Have Happened but Didn't."

Josie was writing about how she found an abandoned baby under a bush in the woods in front of that spooky little house at 800 Boundary Street. The baby turned out to have been stolen by a spaceshipload of extraterrestrials.

After school that day, we were walking in front of 800 Boundary Street on our way to my house as Josie showed me her notes about the baby, the wind blew the notes over the low stone wall into the bushes near the mailbox, and Josie hopped over the wall to get the paper. When she suddenly screamed, "Milly! Look!" I naturally assumed she had found the baby.

But it wasn't a baby. It was jewelry spilling out of a

damp, limp cardboard box. Diamonds sparkled, even in the shade. There were round gold earrings, a diamond and ruby bracelet, a big emerald pin shaped like a beetle, and several other pieces.

"Look at this stuff!" Josie shrieked. "It's like finding buried treasure!"

We examined the jewelry and put it back in the collapsed shipping box as best we could. The muddy label read "Zeena Fovia, 800 Boundary Street."

"It belongs to someone who lives in that spooky house," Josie said. "I wonder what she wants with all this jewelry. Let's take it up there and find out."

"She won't answer the door. She never comes out during the day. I come by here when I deliver papers, and I've never seen her. She gets lots of mail and packages and she doesn't even take them in until after dark. But I've heard people say the lights are on all night. She must be pretty strange."

"So let's come back after dark," Josie said.

Suddenly I heard advice from Aunt Gloria: "Curiosity killed the cat."

I suggested, "Why don't we just leave it on the porch right now? Then we won't have to come back."

"But if we do that, we'll never find out why she wants all this stuff."

More from Aunt Gloria: "Fools walk in where angels fear to tread."

When I didn't say anything, Josie added, "All we're going to do is walk up on the porch, ring the bell, hand her the box, and explain where we found it. If she hasn't eaten us or turned us into vampires or werewolves by then, we'll ask her what she's going to do with all this jewelry. We don't even have to go into the house. Besides, if you lost something, and somebody brought it back, wouldn't you want a chance to say thank you in person?"

"Maybe Uncle Edgar won't let me go." Aunt Gloria wouldn't, that's for sure.

"So ask him," Josie said.

We took the jewelry to my house and showed it to Uncle Edgar.

"Josie thinks we should take the jewelry back to Zeena Fovia tonight."

"I think so, too. I'm sure Zeena would appreciate it."

Josie signaled me a gleeful thumbs-up.

"Do you know Zeena?" I asked Uncle Edgar.

"We went to school together. She and her husband used to live in the big house next to the Jones mansion. When he died a few years ago, she sold the house and most of the furniture and bought that little house in the woods. She's been pretty much of a recluse ever since."

After supper, as it was getting dark, we put the jewelry in a newer box and walked to Boundary Street. I carried the box.

When we got to Zeena Fovia's long, narrow driveway through the woods, we could see light streaming from every window in the tiny one-story house. We made our way up the driveway and onto the front porch.

"I can hear her talking," Josie whispered.

"Me, too. I wonder if she's talking to herself. Ring the bell."

"First I'm going to look in the window."

Josie peered in, then motioned for me to look, too.

Zeena Fovia was sitting at a little table with her back to us, talking on the phone. She was surrounded by stacks of what looked like magazines. Some lay open on the table in front of her; others were piled on the chairs and the floor.

"What are all those magazines?" I whispered to Josie.

Josie cupped her hands around her eyes and peered at the piles closest to the window. "They're not magazines," she whispered with surprise. "They're catalogs!"

Just then Zeena hung up. We jumped away from the window, and Josie rang the bell.

We heard the rustle of movement, and Zeena Fovia opened the door.

She looked disappointingly ordinary — average height, thin, with shiny, dark eyes like a bird's, pointy nose and chin, and shoulder-length black hair. She was wearing jeans and a purple fleece jacket that said L. L. Bean.

"Yes?" she said, peering into the darkness with her little-bird eyes.

Then Josie poked me and I said in one breath, "Mrs. Fovia, we found this jewelry in the woods in front of your house this afternoon and it had your name on it and we thought you might be waiting for it so we decided to bring it to you right away." I held the box out to her.

She studied me for what seemed like a whole minute. Then she began to talk fast, in a thin, twangy voice. The words rushed over Josie and me like water from a broken dam. The torrent almost swept us off the porch, we were so surprised.

"You're Millicent Moore, aren't you? Edgar George's little niece. I used to go to school with Edgar, and of course I knew his brother William and their little sister Anna, your mother, only those two were younger than me, and I always thought Edgar George was one of the nicest people in town, and aren't you lucky to live with him even if it is a funeral parlor, and how is your grandmother? She was always very friendly to all of us children. And your uncle William, how is he? He has a son now, I think, is it Blane? And you have a paper route now, don't you?

"And is this one of your little friends?" she said, turning to Josie.

"Hi, I'm Josie . . ." but before Josie could even say her whole name, the torrent began again.

"Hello, Josie. I'm so pleased to meet you. Won't you two come inside? It's so quiet here at night, and I don't get very much company, but I made some brownies and I was going to put most of them in the freezer, but now that I have somebody to share them with, I guess I won't have to."

Josie and I hesitated. I was still holding the jewelry. Zeena seemed friendly enough. She had said "brownies," which was a magic word as far as Josie and I were concerned. Plus, I was wondering what she might remember about my mother.

So we found ourselves in the little parlor, surrounded by piles of mail order catalogs.

Zeena scurried to the kitchen and came back carrying a plate of brownies on a tray with a carton of milk and some glasses. "Sit down, sit down," she said, but the chairs were full of catalogs.

She put the tray on the floor, in an opening among the stacks, sat cross-legged next to it, and motioned for us to join her. We made a little circle around the brownie tray.

"Now what did you say you found?" she asked me as she picked up a brownie and motioned for us to help ourselves.

I put the box of jewelry on the floor and she looked inside. I explained, "It was in the bushes near the mailbox."

"I was wondering what happened to that," she said. "The delivery man must have left it on the wall instead of bringing it up to the porch. Probably fell in the bushes during that storm the other night. It's so hard keeping track of everything."

She stopped to take a bite of brownie, which created a quiet little island in the rushing river of her conversation. Josie asked, "Where are you going to wear all this jewelry?"

"Oh, I'm not going to wear it at all." She laughed gaily and gulped down her brownie. "It's not real jewelry, of course. It's costume jewelry. But I don't go anyplace where I'd wear *any* jewelry. I just like to order things. I can't sleep at night, so I call the one-eight-hundred numbers and order things from mail order catalogs. Mostly I order clothes. A lot of the catalog companies have people at the phones all night, you know. They're always real friendly. So I chat with them. Then I order merchandise."

She stopped to take another bite.

"But what do you do with all the stuff?" asked Josie.

Zeena hesitated. "Oh, it's in the other room," she said, gesturing vaguely toward the back of the house.

Just then the phone rang and Zeena jumped up to answer it. It must have been an eight-hundred-number person checking on an order: Zeena was talking about colors and sizes.

Josie leaned toward me and whispered, "Zeena Fovia is going to top the Weirdness Index. Do you think maybe we should go?"

"Not yet," I whispered back. "She said she knew Uncle Edgar and my mother when they were little. I never talked to anyone outside the family about my mom. I want to know what she remembers."

"You didn't want to come here in the first place, and now you actually want to stay?"

"You were in such a hurry to come, I can't believe you want to go! You're supposed to be the nosy one.

Don't you want to know what she really does with all the stuff?"

Zeena returned.

She broke off a piece of brownie. "So tell me about you two," she said as she stuffed it in her mouth.

"Well, we had this assignment for English class," I began, "about something that could have happened but didn't—"

By then, Zeena had swallowed. She interrupted, "That sounds interesting. I used to like English class, especially when we were learning how to make speeches."

She took another bite.

While she chewed I said, "And Josie was showing me her notes when we were walking by your woods. And the wind—"

Swallow again. "Do you walk by the woods every day? Don't you think they're lovely?" Bite again.

"Yes, they are. And the wind blew the notes into the bushes and when Josie went to get them—"

Swallow. "And what's your story going to be about, Josie?" Bite.

Josie said, as fast as she could, "It's about finding a baby in the woods. Only we didn't find a baby. We found your jewelry."

Swallow. "A baby! What a clever idea!"

Zeena finally stopped eating to take a drink of milk and Josie gave me a pointed look that meant "What are you waiting for?"

"Mrs. Fovia," I asked quickly, while she gulped, "did

you say you knew Uncle Edgar and my mother when they were little?"

"I sure did. Knew their brother William, too. Your mother was a few years younger than I. A sweet little girl. Always pretending to be a fairy princess or the queen of the world or something. Sometimes I used to baby-sit for her, when Edgar was busy. As a matter of fact—" Suddenly her face lit up the way the big Christmas tree outside the Stone Church did when the minister plugged it in. "Wait right here."

She jumped up and hustled into the next room. As she opened the door we caught a glimpse of piles of boxes, a jumble of furniture, bookcases crammed with books. We heard her rummaging around, muttering to herself.

When Zeena came back, she was blowing the dust off an old scrapbook.

"When I was about fifteen," she said, "I sent away for a camera from a mail order catalog. . . . Even then I loved catalogs!" she added with a laugh. "That summer I took lots and lots of pictures. I think I took some of your mother and her brothers. I never did get very good at it, and after a while the camera broke anyway, but if I took some pictures of the George family, they would be right in this book."

Zeena plunked herself on the floor, spread the book open near the brownie tray, and thumbed through the pages.

"Here they are!" She practically crowed in triumph, turning the book so Josie and I could see the four black-and-white photos held in place by those little black paper corners.

I saw a teenage boy who had to be Uncle Edgar, holding the hand of a fair-haired little girl about seven years old. She was looking up at him with adoration. In another picture the little girl was standing by herself wearing a fairy costume, smiling shyly at the camera. In the third, a young Zeena had her arm around the little girl's shoulder; standing next to Zeena was a teenage boy who had to be Uncle William. In the fourth, the little girl was in a swing, happily pumping toward the sky with her long curls streaming out behind her.

"This is your mother!" Zeena said. "With Edgar and William. And me, of course."

Zeena kept talking, but I stopped listening. I was studying the little girl who lived in that long-ago world of the pictures, trying to imagine what she was like, trying to hear her voice.

Zeena was already curling the photos out of their corner holders.

"Here, you take them," she said matter-of-factly, gently putting the four photos in my hand and patting my hand as she did. "They mean more to you than they do to me."

"Thank you," I whispered.

Josie and I examined my photos while Zeena flipped through the scrapbook again. She fingered the pictures and described them to herself, occasionally laughing out loud.

"Here's one of your aunt Gloria," she said suddenly, and turned the book to show us a pretty, round-faced teenager with blond ringlets. "She and your uncle Edgar were childhood sweethearts, you know."

She flipped the book back and continued to mutter and chuckle to herself.

Suddenly she stopped. "Now I'm not being very polite," she said, closing the book firmly. "I have guests and I'm ignoring them to look at some old scrapbook."

She hesitated, as if she was trying to make up her mind about something. I knew it must be important. This was the first time her voice had stopped all night except for chewing and swallowing.

She stood up abruptly.

"It's good and dark outside," she said. "Let's go for a walk."

Josie and I looked at each other. It was getting late, almost time for Uncle Edgar to drive Josie home. And who waits until it's "good and dark" to go for a walk?

"It won't take long," Zeena said, "and I'll drop you off at the funeral parlor on the way back. Follow me."

She headed toward the back room where she had found the scrapbook.

We hesitated for a second, but then I carefully tucked my photos into a pocket of my jeans, and we followed Zeena through the dusty clutter into another room.

Suddenly we were in a different world. This world was neat and clean. Bright white shelves lined the walls. Orderly piles of new clothing for men, women, and children, all in their original mail-order wrappers, filled the shelves. Sweaters, socks, pants, blouses, T-shirts. The shelves had labels: men's medium, women's 10 petite, girls' 12. A stack of empty shipping cartons stood on a table in the middle of the room.

"Time to make some deliveries," said Zeena. "Each of you pick a carton. Now fill them with whatever you choose. Make sure it's not too heavy to carry. Sometimes I make them too heavy and I can't carry them all the way without stopping for a rest. That's right, just take anything from the shelves. If you want to take all girls' clothes, that's okay. Everything will go eventually."

She continued talking, sometimes to us and sometimes to herself, while we filled our cartons and she piled clothes into another one.

"Leave some room in yours, Milly," she instructed. "We'll put the jewelry in that one."

On the way out the front door, we stopped in the parlor and she added the jewelry to the clothes in my box. On top, she put the big emerald pin that looked like a beetle—for artistic effect, I guessed, because she stepped back and admired it before she closed the box.

She hustled us down wooded Boundary Street, the back way to downtown. Josie and I almost had to run to keep up, leaning backward with the weight of our boxes. Zeena talked all the way, about the clothes we had chosen and the stores they came from and what she would order when she got home.

When we arrived downtown, though, Zeena fell

silent. The last thing she said was, "Shh! We don't want anyone to hear us." We scurried along without a word.

We left Josie's carton on the back steps of the Catholic church. Zeena whispered, "There are lots of poor people in this parish."

We left Zeena's on the porch at the Salvation Army.

We tiptoed past my grandmother's house and left my carton at the back door of the Stone Church. "They're having a flea market here in a few weeks," Zeena explained softly. "They'll make lots of money selling the jewelry."

We walked quickly down my street. In front of our house, Zeena began talking again, still quietly.

"Thanks so much for returning the jewelry, girls, and for joining me on my walk. Please let's keep the deliveries our secret. I hope you'll come visit me again. The next time I'll make chocolate chip cookies, which I usually have on hand anyway, but tonight I decided to make brownies for a change. Please give my very best to your uncle Edgar, and if you ever need anything from a catalog I'll be only too happy to order it for you."

Then she was gone. We heard her muttering as she hustled home.

Josie and I stood still for a while, catching our breath and looking at each other in the light from the front porch. I felt as if I had just gotten off one of those carnival rides that leave you dizzy and disoriented.

Finally, Josie said, "I'm definitely giving Zeena Fovia a nine-point-oh on the Weirdness Index."

"I don't know, Josie. She gave me these great pictures. She knew how much I loved them and I didn't even say a word."

"Maybe I could take some points off for that. Eight-point-five."

"And is it weird to donate nice clothes to poor people and the church?"

"Okay, eight-point-oh."

"And what about the brownies?" I reminded her.

"They were good brownies," Josie admitted. "Seven-point-eight, but not a point lower."

As we went inside, I once again remembered Aunt Gloria telling me that Bentwood had some very peculiar people. I supposed she considered Zeena Fovia one of those peculiar ones. But to me it seemed awfully complicated to figure out who was peculiar and who wasn't.

Josie decided that instead of writing her English paper about finding a baby under a bush in the woods, she'd write about finding a box of jewelry and about the one-eight-hundred lady. Nobody would believe that one, either.

One of a Kind

BLANE TOLD ME if I ever went for a ride with Grandma, I'd surely have an adventure. I had to wait until I was tall enough, though. Grandma thought it was dangerous for anyone under four-feet-six to ride on her Harley-Davidson motorcycle.

A mark on her kitchen doorsill said fifty-four inches. Blane had passed the mark long ago, of course. When I reached it early that fall, Grandma invited me on a weekend trip to Mount Monadnock in New Hampshire.

"We'll take the back roads," she explained, "and see some scenery. On Saturday afternoon, I'm performing a wedding ceremony for a couple of bikers, then I'll preach Sunday morning, and we'll be back Sunday afternoon. If you'd like to come, I'd love to have you."

I had never ridden on a motorcycle. I heard Aunt

Gloria's opinion: "a sure way to get yourself maimed or killed." So I was a little scared. Should I go? Aunt Gloria said: "Over my dead body!" which turned out to be correct, because Uncle Edgar told me, "You decide."

I really wanted a chance to be alone with Grandma. I was saving Zeena Fovia's pictures to show her, as a surprise. I wanted to ask her what my mother was like when she was the little girl in the picture. Whatever else happened, maybe I'd have a chance to talk to Grandma about that.

So, on a bright Friday afternoon early in October, Grandma came to pick me up. Fortunately, no mourners were at the funeral parlor yet. Seeing a tall, silver-haired lady charge up the driveway on a Harley would not contribute to the quiet, peaceful atmosphere people prefer in a funeral parlor.

I checked one last time to make sure my four photos were in my shirt pocket.

I felt a little silly in the black leather jacket Grandma had bought me, with my hair sticking out under the bright red helmet. Grandma said I looked perfect.

As we packed my things next to Grandma's in the saddlebags, Uncle Edgar trimmed the bushes along the driveway. He kept glancing in my direction.

"Edgar, dear, you're hovering," Grandma said kindly. "Relax. We'll be fine."

"I worry about you, going on the road all the time like you do."

"You should know by now that I can take care of

myself." She added, with a grin at me, "And I expect I won't have much trouble taking care of Milly, too, if that's what's really bothering you."

"Ma, you really are one of a kind," he said, shaking his head. I couldn't tell whether he admired that or regretted it; maybe both.

Grandma told me how to sit on the bike, where to put my feet, and where to hold on. With a wave to Uncle Edgar, we were off. I felt like an astronaut being blasted into space, except that the ground never dropped away. In fact, I soon learned that the ground whizzes by very fast and very close when you don't have a car around you to take your mind off it.

After a few minutes, though, I got used to the roar of the engine, leaning at turns, and looking at Grandma's strong, straight back, the only object that remained steady as the world zoomed past.

Of course, I had told Josie about Grandma and the weekend trip. The road out of town went past her parents' store, and Josie was watching for us from the parking lot.

When we approached, she waved. As we flew by, she held up a big cardboard sign: "7.0." At least Grandma and I were scoring lower than Zeena.

Grandma called back, "What's that all about?"

"Nothing," I hollered. "It's just Josie. Too complicated to explain."

It seemed to me that we were moving awfully fast. But when we came up behind Angus MacDonald in his antique Studebaker, we had to slow down so much

I was afraid we'd tip over. Grandma soon sped up again, though, and we made a loop around Angus and gave him a wave. Then we were out of town and on our way.

From time to time, we stopped to admire the view. After a few hours, we parked at a place called Scenic Lookout to watch the hills change color in the glow of the sunset.

Then we whooshed down a darkening wooded road and pulled in near a loud sign that said "Scenic Look-out Motel" in bright yellow lights above a long row of tiny, neat cottages. A cheerful restaurant gave off the sound of taped organ music and the smell of frying hamburgers.

The few diners didn't pay much attention when we walked in, but the short, smiling, round man behind the counter boomed through his bushy gray beard, "Well, Sarah. Long time no see! On your way to Mount Monadnock? And who is this little waif?"

"This is my granddaughter, Milly. Milly, this is Nick, but most people call him Santa. I suppose you can guess why."

Grandma arranged for a room in Santa's motel; then we picked a table and ordered supper.

I gobbled down my burger and fries. Grandma was gobbling, too, and we didn't talk much as we ate. But while we waited for dessert, I said, "I have something to show you." I took the photos out of my pocket and spread them on the table.

"These are wonderful, Milly! Where did you get them?" she exclaimed, examining them one by one.

"Zeena Fovia gave them to me."

"Of course! This is Zeena right here, with Anna and William!" She thought for a second. "That must have been the summer your mother was about seven."

"What was she like when she was seven?"

Grandma smiled, remembering. "She was very imaginative. Always playing dress-up, singing little songs that she made up. She adored Edgar. And William, too. They were quite a bit older than she, though."

"What was she like when she was my age? Was she like me?"

"You look a little like her. And sometimes you remind me of her."

"How?"

"She liked to read stories. She worked hard in school. She was sort of quiet. She wasn't quite as shy as you are sometimes, though."

At first, as we were eating and talking, I had only half-noticed the raggedy-looking man hunched over a cup of coffee in the corner booth. But after a while, I realized that he was staring at Grandma and me.

"Grandma, don't look now, but that man's staring at us."

Grandma didn't look right then, but soon she thought up some reason to turn around and gave him a glance.

"Poor scrawny thing," she said. "He seems pretty young to look so miserable and unhappy."

"Why's he staring at us?"

"I don't know. But don't worry about it," she said matter-of-factly, and she went back to looking at the pictures.

I told her, "Zeena has a picture of Aunt Gloria when she was a teenager, too. She said Gloria and Uncle Edgar were childhood sweethearts."

"That's right. They weren't very much alike, but they were always fond of each other. All Gloria ever wanted was to marry Edgar and be a housewife. She was very prim and proper. And she had very strong opinions about the right way to do things."

"*That* sure didn't change when she grew up." I happened to know quite a lot about Aunt Gloria's strong opinions.

Grandma smiled. "Maybe you couldn't always tell, but Gloria was quite fond of you."

"She was? But she never let me do anything!"

"She was always afraid something bad might happen to you. And she wanted you to be just like her, which is natural enough. But of course you're not like her. You're not just like your mother, either. People are way too complicated for any two of us to be alike."

She added, "Just between you and me, I always felt a little sorry for Gloria. She was so sure about the right way to be that she could never really enjoy people who weren't that way. And the world is full of interesting people who aren't."

"She used to say they were peculiar people."

"Exactly."

"I wonder if she considered *me* a peculiar person."

"Maybe. I'm sure she considered *me* one." Grandma laughed.

When we finished dessert, I put the photos back in my shirt pocket and we went to our cabin. Before long, I was snuggled in the bed near the wall and Grandma was getting into the bed near the door. I fell asleep as soon as she turned the light off.

The faint creak of the front window being opened during the night woke me up.

At first, I thought I was having a bad dream. I blinked my eyes to make sure I was awake. Then I froze. By the glow of the yellow lights outside, I could see a man climbing in the window carefully and silently. It was that raggedy guy from the restaurant, the young man who had been staring at Grandma and me.

Aunt Gloria always told me that if there's an intruder in your room, it's best to pretend you're asleep. I was so scared my muscles wouldn't move if I told them to! But if I closed my eyes, I'd have to imagine what he was doing. That would be more scary than watching and knowing. So I left them open just a slit. I thought about Aunt Gloria not wanting anything bad to happen to me. Maybe I shouldn't have come! I wished Josie was here instead of me. She probably wouldn't be so scared. She'd probably start tallying up how to rate this experience on her Weirdness Index or thinking up a million questions to ask this creepy man.

Step by careful step, he tiptoed to the little table near the foot of my bed. He began to rummage through Grandma's handbag. If he came one inch closer I'd have to scream.

I didn't know whether to hope Grandma would stay asleep or hope she would wake up.

But suddenly, with one enormous leap, Grandma was out of bed, the light was on, and she was standing tall in her flowery pajamas, demanding, "Excuse me, but exactly what do you think you're doing?"

The man snatched the handbag and ran for the door, but Grandma was too fast for him. Flowered arms and legs flying, she jumped across her bed and grabbed his arm. There was a scuffle. The next thing I knew, he was lying flat on his back on the floor. Grandma was practically sitting on his chest. He was moaning, "You broke my nose, you broke my nose."

"I'm sorry you bumped your nose. I'm sure it's not broken," she said kindly but forcefully.

"Grandma, you want me to call Santa and tell him to get the police?"

"No. Wet a towel with cold water and bring it here."

"But, Grandma, he could have killed you!"

"I'm okay. I don't believe he meant to hurt either one of us. Did you?" she asked him. It was more a statement than a question. He shook his head frantically.

I got the towel and Grandma gently pressed it to

his nose while he stared at her in fear and disbelief.

"I'm going to let you get up," she said, "if you think you can behave yourself."

He nodded anxiously.

Before she got off his chest, she preached him a sermonette. "I suppose you think that because you need money, it's okay just to take it. But in the long run, that approach will never work. I imagine you thought it would be easy to rob an old lady and a little girl. As you can see, that approach doesn't work so well either."

Then she got off him. "Get up and sit down."

She motioned toward the chair next to the little table, the only chair in the room. He sat erect on the edge of it, holding the towel to his nose, glancing nervously between Grandma and me. He was shorter than Grandma, pale and thin, with dark, matted hair. His jeans and flannel shirt were rumpled and dirty; he smelled sweaty.

I sat on my bed. Grandma sat on hers.

She looked him straight in the eye—with that look that can see into people's hearts—and demanded quietly, "Now suppose you tell me what this is all about. First, what's your name?"

"Alan." He spoke so softly I could hardly hear him.

"Alan what?"

"Alan Brown."

By this sort of question and answer, she dragged his story out of him. He had been a handyman for some rich people near Philadelphia, but he lost the job when they sold their estate. He had hitchhiked to New Hampshire because he heard about a similar job up here, but somebody else got it. He had run out of money and had been sleeping in the woods, and he'd used his last bit of change that night to buy coffee at Santa's.

Grandma picked up the phone and dialed. She waited. "I'm sorry to wake you, Nick, but we have a situation here. Would you mind meeting us in the kitchen?"

I put my clothes on over my pajamas, and she did the same. We all arrived in the restaurant just as a sleepy Santa was turning on the lights.

He raised his eyebrows in mild surprise to see that we had a guest. He looked questioningly at Grandma, but he didn't say anything. It was almost as if he half expected Grandma to get him up in the middle of the night to be kind to a ragged stranger.

"We have someone here who needs something to eat," Grandma said.

Santa nodded and turned to the grill.

"Milly," she said, "why don't you and Alan go sit down while I have a chat with Nick."

I chose a table and we sat across from each other. I didn't have any idea what to say to a guy who had just tried to rob us. But Aunt Gloria had always told me that children shouldn't speak until spoken to, a rule that was coming in handy at the moment. After all, Alan was the grown-up in this situation—even if he was a thief.

He looked around nervously at the ceiling, the floor, and the other tables. He fiddled with the salt shaker.

"Is that your grandmother?" he asked finally.

"Yeah."

"Do you think she's going to turn me in to the police?"

"I don't know. Probably not. She could have done that already if she wanted to."

"What's she going to do?"

"First I guess she's going to get you something to eat."

Nick brought us each a cup of hot chocolate and placed a huge plate of scrambled eggs, bacon, and toast in front of Alan.

"Thank you," Alan mumbled, and dug into his meal. He practically inhaled it. I sipped my hot chocolate.

Grandma and Nick were still talking in the kitchen when Alan mopped up the last speck of egg with his last piece of toast.

He leaned back in his chair and sighed. "That was great," he said. He folded his hands across his stomach as if he could feel it full from the outside as well as the inside.

"Where are you and your grandmother from?"

I told him we were from Massachusetts, and where we were going and why.

"You mean she rides a motorcycle? A grandmother who's a minister and rides a motorcycle? What's the rest of your family like?"

So I told him about Uncle Edgar and Aunt Gloria and Blane. I showed him my photos. He said things like "nice family" and "too bad about your mother" and asked me what it was like to live in a funeral parlor.

Finally, Grandma came to the table.

"Nick's going to let you stay in one of his cabins tonight," she announced, "and tomorrow he'll see what he can do. He said he could use some help around here, so maybe he'll have a job for you."

"Thank you," Alan said quietly. "Thank you for everything. I'm sorry for all the trouble I caused."

"Glad to help. And I don't want to hear about you trying to rob any more helpless little old ladies."

"No, ma'am, you sure won't."

We all went out, and Nick turned off the lights. Grandma and I went to our cabin, and Santa unlocked another for Alan.

"Night, Milly," Alan called softly as he went in.

Grandma and I went back to bed. She conked right out. But I had trouble getting to sleep. My brain was too busy trying to sort everything out: how Grandma had been so brave, how she and Nick were kind to a guy who tried to rob us, how the man who had seemed so creepy and scary at first turned out to be pitiful and even sort of nice. . . .

The next afternoon, while Grandma was "uniting this man and this woman in holy matrimony," I remembered what she said about Aunt Gloria and me. Aunt Gloria had been doing her best to make me into

Gloria the Second. But it wasn't working. I was me—not like anybody else, not even like my own mother.

Sunday morning, I watched Grandma preach to the bikers on the mountainside. I thought proudly that nobody in the world was entirely like my grandmother. Uncle Edgar had been right when he called her "one of a kind."

Blane had been right, too, when he said I'd surely have an adventure if I went for a ride with Grandma. I couldn't wait to tell Josie all about it. She had already scored Grandma and me seven-point-oh on the Weirdness Index. I wondered how many points we'd get for an actual robber.

Uncle Edgar's Reject Party

EVERY DAY for two weeks, Josie dashed home from school and tore through the mailbox, hoping to find the engraved invitation that never came.

Carol Jones was giving a Gala Halloween Ball at the Jones mansion. Some of us had to face the fact that our names wouldn't appear on the invitation list. By Friday afternoon of the second week, even Josie had given up.

"It's going to be such a great party," she moaned as we sat in my bedroom after school. "I heard Carol talking about it in the girls' room. They're decorating the living room and dining room like an old-fashioned ballroom. Everybody's going dressed like kings and queens or rich movie stars and rock stars. I wanted to go as Cleopatra being bitten by the asp. They're having a deejay and everything. I'd give anything to be invited."

"Some other kids weren't invited either, in case you hadn't noticed."

"But you don't even like to dress up."

"Maybe I wouldn't mind just this once, if it meant I got to see what a real ball is like. Just out of curiosity."

I figured we couldn't count on some bossy fairy godmother popping out of nowhere to get us to *this* ball. Too bad Aunt Gloria wasn't here. She'd *love* a gala ball at the Joneses; it would be so proper and perfect. *She'd* get us there whether we wanted to go or not.

I ripped open the big bag of M&Ms that Uncle Edgar had given me and offered some to Josie. We devoured the whole bagful. As we ate, I thought out loud, "Too bad we can't have a party ourselves. We could invite all the kids who aren't going to Carol's."

"Yeah, too bad," Josie said. "But my mom's too busy with the little kids on Halloween to have a party at our house."

We munched in gloomy silence.

Suddenly Josie sat erect. "Joyabounding!" she exclaimed. "Maybe your Uncle Edgar would let us have a party here!"

"Here? We've never had a party here! Besides, you're my only friend who ever comes here. Everybody else thinks it's too creepy."

"Think about it! What better place is there for a Halloween party than a place that's already creepy?"

"Do you really think the kids would come?"

"Look at it this way. Would you rather go to a party at a creepy place, or not go to a party at all?"

That night, while Uncle Edgar and I ate supper, I told him all about Carol Jones's party.

"Josie and I were wondering if maybe we could have a party here on the same night."

"I don't know, Milly," he said in that slow deliberate way of his. "How many kids do you think there would be?"

"Maybe ten including us."

He scrunched his eyebrows. He was thinking it over. I knew enough not try to talk him into it. He liked to say "yes" to me whenever he could.

Then I noticed just the hint of a sly little grin on his face. I had never seen that particular grin before. "I suppose there's no better place to have a Halloween party than a funeral parlor," he said.

The next day Josie, Uncle Edgar, and I held a planning session for what Uncle Edgar was cheerfully calling the Reject Party.

If the Gala Halloween Ball was having a deejay, we would have our stereo system that Uncle Edgar uses for organ music at viewings. If the Jones's dining room and living room were decorated like a ballroom, we would decorate our viewing room like—well, like a viewing room, with a casket, flowers, and dim lights to make everything spooky. And our house had rooms the Joneses couldn't dream of in their fancy mansion.

Carol had invited all the rich kids to her ball. Most of the kids at the Reject Party wouldn't be able to afford expensive costumes. Josie and I got Blane to help us design an invitation on the computer. It showed a bloody-faced vampire in a coffin sneering, "Come to this party. If you dare. Homemade costumes only. Or else."

Josie and I assembled our costumes. I was going in dark brown pants and a dark brown shirt. Uncle Edgar let me have a package of labels he used for the file folders in his office. I looked through the dictionary for the longest words I could find, wrote one on each label, and stuck the labels all over the shirt. I borrowed a dark brown scarf from Uncle Edgar and wrapped it around my head. Uncle Edgar had an old pair of glasses with round, thick, black frames; one lens was missing, and he took the other one out for me. I put my library card in a plastic bag to tie around my neck with a brown ribbon.

"What do you think?" I asked Josie, modeling my costume in my room one afternoon.

"What the heck *are* you?"

I took a book off the shelf and pretended to read.

"A bookworm!" she exclaimed. "That's great!"

Now Josie wanted to be the ghost of a fairy tale princess who had been decapitated by a wicked ogre. She had enlisted her mother's help to put on eyeliner, dark lipstick, chalky white makeup, and a blood-red lipstick line around her neck to show the mark of the ogre's deadly slice.

"The only problem is," she said, "I can't decide what to do for a dress. I don't have anything fancy enough for a fairy tale princess."

Joyabounding, I had the perfect dress.

I opened my closet, pushed to the very back, and pulled out the frilly pink dress I had worn for Aunt Gloria's viewing.

"How's this to start with?" I said, holding it up for Josie.

"Wow! What a great dress!"

"You actually *like* it? I hate this dress. I feel silly in it."

"You can be so weird sometimes, Milly. Where did you get it?"

"Aunt Gloria made it."

"Are you sure it's okay if I wear it to the party?"

"It's okay with me."

We thought it would look more like a fairy tale princess dress if we pinned Christmas tree tinsel all over it. So that's what we did.

Our party was planned for Friday night. On Thursday afternoon, as I was coming in the front door after school, Charles Harkness from across the street was going out. He smiled shyly and, I thought, a little sadly as we passed.

I had never seen him outside the bank on a regular working day.

"How come Charles Harkness was here?" I asked Uncle Edgar in his office.

Uncle Edgar looked at me as if he couldn't decide what to say.

"His mother died early this morning."

"That's too bad. I didn't even know he had a mother. She must have been pretty old."

"She was ninety-five. Hetty and Martha's older sister. But she's been in a nursing home for years. You've never met her.

"Milly," he continued carefully, "the funeral is going to be on Saturday. That means we have to have the viewing tomorrow."

Tomorrow! The night of the party!

"What are we going to do?"

"I've been giving this a lot of thought since Charles called me this morning. I thought we'd have to cancel the party. In fact, if it had been anybody but Charles Harkness, I would have decided to do that immediately."

Uncle Edgar talked calmly and slowly like always. I tried to be calm, but my insides were churning! How could I ever tell Josie there would be no party?

"But I've been friends with Charles all my life," he continued. "I decided to talk it over with him. I told him what we had planned, and why. First, he said we could hold the viewing earlier, so it would be over before eight when your friends get here. I told him we could confine the party to the basement, since of course his mother will still be in the viewing room. But he said Halloween used to be his mother's favorite holiday and she'd be delighted to be at the party. What do you think?"

I didn't know what to think. Everybody expects some creepiness on Halloween. But would having an actual dead person at the party make it too far beyond creepy? I wanted to have the party more than anything! I wanted my school friends to come to our house. I wanted them to meet Uncle Edgar. I didn't want to disappoint Josie.

"I guess I think we should do it."

The next night around eight, one of the men who helped Uncle Edgar with funerals stood at the end of our front walk, wearing his formal black suit. He directed the kids to the back door. There another of Uncle Edgar's helpers, in his black suit and a skeleton mask, pointed wordlessly down the dark stairs that led to the basement.

Downstairs, the kids were greeted by somber organ music. Uncle Edgar waited, in a long black coat and top hat like an old-fashioned funeral director. A bookworm holding a book of stories called *Spine Tinglers* introduced each guest to Uncle Edgar, and he quietly invited them to go into the showroom.

In the showroom, a few candles on top of the closed caskets lit the room dimly, reflecting off the polished surfaces and faintly illuminating gauzy, ghostly figures hanging from the ceiling.

Josie floated around eerily as her decapitated princess. Dim and Dimmer wore one enormous, ragged, faded T-shirt. Dim's left leg and Dimmer's right leg were tied together so they could organize their footsteps: They were a (short) two-headed giant. One of the boys, a neighbor of Josie's, was draped in a fifty-pound rabbit-food sack with a scoop on a string around his neck. One of the girls wore a floor-length, straight, white dress and a crumpled aluminum foil hat; she was a tooth with a filling.

Flora, who had closed the flower shop tonight to help with the party, was dressed in a long black robe. Her face was painted bone white; her red hair poked out from a black hood. She stood at the antique coffin, silently offering sodas from the cooler inside.

The kids peered at her with curiosity as they took their drinks. They clustered in little groups, glancing warily at the caskets and the ghosts. They spoke in murmurs, when they could think of anything to say. The words I heard most often were "creepy" and "spooky" followed by "weird."

Josie whispered happily, "This room looks really spooky and weird. I didn't know you were going to make all those creepy ghosts!"

"I didn't make them. Uncle Edgar must have done it without telling me. I wonder what else he didn't tell me."

Uncle Edgar spoke above the whispering. In the casket-surrounded darkness, his deep, soft voice sounded sinister. "Good evening, and welcome to the Edgar George Funeral Parlor. In a few minutes, we'll go upstairs. But first, we thought you might like a tour.

"We call this room the showroom. As you can see, this is our collection of caskets. Would you like to see inside one of them?"

Without waiting for an answer, he ceremoniously removed the candle from the top of one of the caskets and handed it to Flora. Slowly, he opened the casket.

We all moved closer for a better look. Inside lay a full-size skeleton. It was wearing a white shirt, blue necktie, and glasses. Its hands were clasped across its chest.

"Oops," said Uncle Edgar sadly, "I guess we forgot someone. That happens sometimes." He left the casket open.

"Would you like to see the embalming room now?" he asked.

Nobody knew what to say.

We followed him across the hall. He turned on only one dim wall light in the embalming room.

Peering into the gray darkness, I couldn't believe I was seeing what I was seeing. I blinked.

The figure of a man dressed in a business suit lay dead still on the embalming table. His face seemed distorted and scarred.

"This poor gentleman," Uncle Edgar explained, "died in a horrible accident." Uncle Edgar began to explain what funeral directors do in an embalming room, how they take fluids out of the body and replace them with preservatives.

By this time, our eyes had grown used to the darkness.

Suddenly, Josie screamed, "He moved! I saw his fingers move!"

"Where?" we all said.

"His right hand! His fingers were twitching!"

Uncle Edgar was calm. He said kindly, "I don't think so. This man has been dead for several days."

He continued his lecture about embalming. But who was listening? We were all staring at the man's right hand.

When Uncle Edgar turned to take one of his surgical tools off the table, the man's elbow bent suddenly and his hand popped up. We all shouted, "He's moving! He's moving!"

By the time Uncle Edgar looked, the hand was down again and motionless.

"I'm afraid you're letting your imaginations run away with you," he said patiently. "Let's turn on the light and you'll see that this man is really dead."

As he turned his back to pull the string of the overhead light, the dead man suddenly sat bolt upright. We all gasped—ten kids, one gasp.

Slowly the man reached for Uncle Edgar's neck with both hands.

"Look out!" someone screamed.

Uncle Edgar turned around. He was face to face with the dead man.

"No!" he bellowed.

The dead man leaped off the table and ran for the door.

By now we were all hollering. We scrambled to get out of his way. He disappeared down the hall.

We looked at Uncle Edgar. With a shaky hand, he pulled the string to turn on the light. His eyes were wide with fright.

Slowly, he began to smile.

His smile grew wider and wider.

"Sorry about that, folks," he grinned. "We just couldn't resist. Let me introduce you to our dead man. Mr. Charles Harkness."

The dead man walked back into the room, pulled off his rubber mask, and said quietly, "Hello, everybody."

All the kids began talking at once. "That was great!" "I knew from the beginning it was a trick!" "I thought he was really dead!"

Josie said, "I was petrified! That was fantastic!"

I felt a happy rush of affection for Uncle Edgar. "I didn't know you were an actor," I said. "How come you didn't tell me you were going to do all this?"

"And spoil the surprise?"

When the kids quieted down again, Uncle Edgar said seriously, "We'll go upstairs for the rest of the party. First, though, I have to explain something. This part is no joke. We've had a viewing here today, and the funeral will be tomorrow. So when you get off the elevator, you'll see a lady in her casket. That lady is Mr. Harkness's mother."

No one said a word. He led us to the elevator and explained why it was long and thin, and we all piled in. It was so quiet when we got off the elevator that even the solemn organ music seemed loud and boisterous.

Uncle Edgar and Charles Harkness led us into the viewing room. The kids stepped cautiously, hanging back. Tiny, wrinkled Mrs. Harkness lay on pale pink pillows in a mahogany casket, wearing a lavender dress with a pink rose at its neck. A pink and white floral arrangement with a ribbon reading "Mother" lay across the bottom half of the casket. A basket of yellow and white gladiolus saying "Sister" stood near the head of the casket; another saying "Friend" stood at its foot. In the soft spotlights, Mrs. Harkness appeared to be sleeping.

Uncle Edgar said, "Mr. Harkness has something he would like to say to you."

Charles's eyes flitted among us. He said softly, "My mother loved Halloween. She had a party every year when I was young. Her favorite part of the party was a scary skit she'd put on with some of us to help her. I don't know if she can see us or not, but she would have loved our skit downstairs. She'd be thrilled to be at this party, and she'd want you all to have a wonderful time."

Before anyone had a chance to wonder whether this was way too creepy, Uncle Edgar asked, "Who wants to help me pick out some music?"

He put regular music on the sound system. Flora fluttered in from the kitchen with Halloween cookies and a special drink she called Blood Red Punch.

Everybody was suddenly starved. Pretty soon the kids were gobbling up the cookies and telling each other scary stories. We were all talking at once and laughing. Uncle Edgar answered a hundred questions about funerals and dead people. Dim and Dimmer got up their courage to talk with Charles Harkness because, as it turned out, they both wanted to be bank tellers. Flora bustled around and even got Uncle Edgar to dance with her. They did an old dance called the twist that involved wiggling and shaking all over. We thought it was hilarious. They insisted that we all learn how to do it, too.

The kids kept stealing glances at Mrs. Harkness until they got used to her being there. To me, it seemed right to have somebody's mother at our party, even if we couldn't exactly tell whether she was having a good time. Whenever I looked at her, though, I thought she looked happy.

I hadn't heard from Aunt Gloria lately. I couldn't help wondering what she would say about all this—probably "What will the neighbors think?" But there *was* our neighbor, Charles Harkness, chatting cordially with the twins and drinking Flora's bloody punch, right next to his mother in her casket, so I guess you can't always live your life by what the neighbors might say.

At eleven, when it was time to leave, Uncle Edgar and I stood at the door to say good-bye. Uncle Edgar shook Dim's right hand and Dimmer's left. "Oh, wait," the twins said together. They hobbled on their three legs to the casket. "Good-bye, Mrs. Harkness," said Dim. Dimmer added, "We're glad you came to the party."

All the kids filed by the casket to say good-bye to Mrs. Harkness.

As Josie left, she told Uncle Edgar, "I've never been to such a great party."

Charles Harkness said, "And I've never been to such a great viewing."

When everyone was gone, I hugged Uncle Edgar. "That was so much fun! It was perfect! I should call Carol Jones right now and tell her she's wonderful for not inviting us to her ball. Thank you for everything, Uncle Edgar."

"I should thank you and Josie for the idea, Milly. I haven't had that much fun since Gloria and I were teenagers."

The Reject kids talked about our party for weeks. Josie was thrilled to overhear Carol's friend Ashley say that everyone who had gone to Carol's party was wishing they'd been at ours instead. It was true they had all been invited to a fancy ball. But not one of them had ever been to a Halloween party with a real live dead person.

At the Left-Brain/ Right-Brain Bookstore

IT WAS LATE at night. Flora, Josie, Blane, and I sat silently in a semicircle of beanbag chairs in the dark and quiet right-brain half of the Left-Brain/Right-Brain Bookstore. We peered into the shadows, waiting for something to happen.

When Bob and Gracie Arnold had bought this old two-story house and remodeled it into the Left-Brain/Right-Brain Bookstore, I asked Uncle Edgar about brains. Uncle Edgar knew a lot about how people work, even though he mainly dealt with them after they stopped working.

He explained that a person's brain has two halves. The left side is logical and analytical. It likes facts, numbers, and order. The right side is more intuitive. It cares more about how ideas relate to each other than what order they're in. The right brain likes art, music, and spirituality. Some people operate more in the left-brain mode; some people like their right brain better. Computer-genius Blane was way left-brained. Joyabounding Flora was way right-brained. I guessed Josie and I were somewhere in the middle.

Sitting in the right-brain half of the bookstore, Gracie's half, we could see, by the dim light of the street lamp, books scattered in no particular order, on shelves, the floor, and little tables. ("This place is a mess," Blane whispered.) I knew that the only labeled shelf said "Books I Really Like." When the lights were on, the odd assortment of table lamps and floor lamps gave the room a warm homey glow. If customers wanted to pay for a book, they had to go find Gracie, who was usually curled up on a beanbag chair, engrossed in her reading, her long, flowery skirt wrapped around her bare toes.

The left-brain bookstore across the hall, Bob's half, was arranged like a library, with books shelved according to subject and then alphabetically by author. A square wooden table and four heavy chairs sat exactly in the middle of the room. When the store was open, fluorescent lights gave the left-brain bookstore a cool bluish tinge. Blane worked for Bob after school. He had designed the computer system Bob used to keep track, in excruciatingly minute detail, of his customers' book-buying habits.

That morning, Gracie had gone next door to the flower shop, to ask Flora what she should do about some weird, mysterious happenings in her right-brain half of the bookstore. I was at the shop picking up flowers for Uncle Edgar. Blane was there, too, balancing Flora's checkbook, as he did every week.

Flora's shop had one room for a normal flower business, and another room for incense and crystals and fortune-telling stuff, with spacey music on the CD player. If you didn't know what to do about weird happenings at your house, Flora was the one to ask.

"I don't know what to think," Gracie said to us. "When we're in bed upstairs at night, we hear bumps and thumps from my side of the store, but when we look, nobody's there. In the morning, books are lined up on the shelves, in order, alphabetized—not at all the way I left them."

"It sounds to me," Flora said, "as if you have some disturbed spirit in your house. It could be the ghost of someone who has died; maybe some poor unfortunate who can't rest in peace because he or she is upset about something. Sometimes they rearrange things to get people's attention."

"What should we do?" Gracie asked.

"Here's what I'd suggest, if Milly is willing to help."

"Me?" I jumped. I couldn't imagine how *I* could help with a *ghost*.

"It's well known," Flora explained, "that some girls your age attract psychic energy. You might see or hear something that will give us a clue to what's going on. Don't be nervous. I'll be there to tell you what to do."

I hesitated. "Well, I guess I could try." I was surprised to find myself thinking that if there was a ghost, I might like to see it. "Could Josie come, too? *She's* my age." Josie would never forgive me if I got a chance to see a ghost and didn't take her.

"Yes, of course. And you, Blane. Would you come? You're so level-headed and logical, you'll be perfect as an objective observer."

So there we were, the four of us, waiting in the lonely, quiet dark. Bob and Gracie were spending the night somewhere else, as Flora had advised.

"Nothing's happening," Blane whispered. "I'm sure there's a perfectly natural explanation for what's been going on."

"We just have to be patient and wait and see," Flora said, in a calming, in-control voice very unlike her usual fluttery self.

We waited some more. Nothing but quiet, an occasional car passing outside, the sound of our breathing.

Suddenly, I thought I heard a new sound.

"Shh! I hear something."

"What?" they all whispered.

"It's like a slow thump . . . thump . . . thump. But very faint."

"Does anyone else hear it?" Flora asked. They both said no.

"Stay relaxed, Milly," she said gently. "Unfocus your mind so you're not trying to see or hear anything in particular. Let whatever happens happen."

I took a deep breath. I tried to relax and unfocus. The thumping continued. Gradually it grew a little louder.

Then I heard a faraway unsteady hum, almost like someone speaking over a very bad phone connection.

"I hear something else now. I think it sounds like a voice!"

"Can you make out any words?"

I waited.

"No, it's too blurry. Just a sound here and there. But it's definitely a voice."

I listened.

"I feel as if someone's trying very hard to tell me something, but I just can't understand what it is."

"Relax and be patient," Flora said.

As my ears and eyes strained into the darkness, I thought I saw something move.

A book, all by itself, slid along a shelf and came to rest against another book. Thump.

"Did anybody see that?" I asked.

"What?"

"The book moved!"

Another book floated up from the floor and tucked itself onto the shelf next to the first. Thump.

"Oh, my gosh, I saw a book move!" If a person could scream and whisper at the same time, Josie was doing it.

A third book drifted off a table and slid into place next to the second.

"Did you see that, Josie?" I asked.

"Yes, I did!"

I heard a gasp. It was Blane. "I don't believe this! I see books moving!"

"Shh! The voice is getting a little clearer," I whispered.

We watched in silence as the books continued to straighten themselves out.

"It sounds like an old man's voice, kind of crackly and weak."

I listened.

"I can hear him now. He's saying, 'This place is a mess, this place is a mess.' Can you hear him?"

They all said no. I listened some more.

"He's saying something else now. 'Where's my picture? Where's my picture?' "

"Keep your eyes unfocused, Milly," Flora coached, "as if you're looking far into the distance. Can you see anything?"

The bookstore was dark. But as I watched, a patch of gray appeared, as if a bit of fog had drifted in.

Gradually, it began to take shape.

"I'm starting to see a person!"

"Does anybody else see anything?" Flora asked.

Blane said, "Books moving!"

Josie said, "I see something like a gray cloud."

"It's an old man, with shaggy white hair." I could see at last. "He's picking books up and putting them on the shelves. And muttering about the mess and his picture."

After a few minutes, the man began to fade. The muttering stopped. No more books moved.

The four of us were alone again in the quiet dark.

"He's gone," I said.

Flora turned the lamp on. We blinked in the bright light and stared at each other.

"Wow," Josie said at last, "that sure was spooky!"

"Milly, you did a wonderful job," Flora said.

Blane was in shock. "I can't believe it! The books moved!"

"What should we do now?" I asked.

"Let's think a minute," said Flora, "about who that poor old man might be, and what might be bothering him."

Blane quickly snapped back to his usual logical self. "Well," he said, "let's assume for a minute that there really was a ghost. And let's assume, for now, that he really did say something. The first thing he said made perfect sense. He said this place is a mess. He's right. It is a mess, and he was straightening it out. Second, he was looking for a picture. Can anybody figure out what that means?"

"Whatever it is, it's connected with this house," said Flora. "Ghosts stay attached to a place that was important to them when they were alive. He expects some picture to be where he used to have it, and he's worried that it's missing. If we could find it, maybe he'd be able to rest in peace."

"How would we know where to look?" I asked. I thought about the wedding picture on my desk at home, and the old photographs that Zeena Fovia had given me. Maybe pictures could mean a lot even to a ghost.

"We wouldn't," said Flora, "unless it happens to be in the house somewhere."

Blane said, "Bob told me that when they moved in here, there was all kinds of old furniture and stuff. They saved some of it in the cellar and the attic. Maybe there were some pictures."

"We should definitely see if we can find some," I said.

"Logically," Blane added, "Bob would have put the heaviest stuff in the cellar and the lightest stuff in the attic. So let's look in the attic."

Blane knew where Bob kept a flashlight and the keys to the attic, so he got them and we climbed the narrow stairway. Blane shone the light around the cramped space, on packing boxes stacked neatly along the walls.

We examined each box in the narrow beam of light. Finally, we saw one marked "Pictures: Front Office."

"Let's try that one," said Blane.

There was room for only two of us to crouch in the tiny space near the box. Blane opened it, and he and I examined the framed pictures one by one. Each photo showed groups of people smiling into the camera. One man appeared in every photo. In the first ones we looked at, he was very young. As we examined the photos and laid them aside, he grew older and older.

Suddenly I realized: "That's the old man I saw downstairs!"

Blane handed the picture and the flashlight to Flora.

"Why, that's James Peterson!" said Flora. "This used

to be his house. He was an accountant, and that front room on the right side of the house was his office. In fact, I think that's where he died."

Blane said, "Accountants work with numbers all the time. They're pretty left-brained. I guess James Peterson probably wouldn't like the right-brain bookstore very much. He'd like everything neat and orderly."

"No wonder he can't rest in peace," I said.

Josie said, "That explains what he said about the mess, and why he was moving the books. But how do we know what picture he was talking about?"

As Flora held the picture, I could see that the back was labeled, in very careful black block lettering. They were all labeled.

Blane and I went through the photos again, reading the labels. They said things like "With Mayor and City Manager 1985," "At Association Awards Dinner 1973," and "With Chamber of Commerce Officers 1967."

Finally, we came to one that said "With Mother and Father at Graduation 1928." It showed a young, smiling James Peterson standing between a man and woman who looked happy and proud.

"This is the one," I said.

"How do you know?" Blane asked.

"It's his parents. I just know this is the one."

We put the other photos back in the packing box and carried Mr. Peterson and his parents downstairs to the right-brain bookstore.

"If Milly's right," said Blane, "at least we know what

picture he's talking about. But we still don't know what to do with it."

"And the other thing that's bothering him," I said, "is that his old office is messy. He won't be at peace until he gets it straightened out."

"And Gracie won't be at peace if he ever *does* get it straightened out," said Blane.

Josie asked, "So what do we do?"

"Usually when a ghost is bothering people," Flora explained, "you bring in a psychic who convinces him that he's dead and doesn't belong among the living anymore. Then he goes away."

"I don't think straightening things up in the middle of the night is such a bother," Josie said. "I wish I had a ghost like that in my room at home."

"Logically, there's only one thing to do," said Blane.

"What's that?" we asked.

"Switch sides."

"Joyabounding!" Josie and I said at the same time.

The next day, we explained our discovery to Bob and Gracie. Josie, Blane, and I helped them move everything in the left-brain bookstore to the right side of the house. We moved everything in the right-brain bookstore to the left side of the house. We hung the photograph of James Peterson with his mother and father in a special spot on the wall opposite the door to the new left-brain bookstore.

Bob nailed a sign to the front door of the house: "To

view the Left-Brain/Right-Brain Bookstore from the proper perspective, please use the back door."

Mr. Peterson must have been more at peace in his new surroundings where everything was neat and alphabetical and he could see his family photo, because there were no more bumps in the night. But Gracie said that if the left-brain bookstore ever did need some straightening up, at least Bob would appreciate the help.

Josie gave the Left-Brain/Right-Brain Bookstore eight-point-five on the Weirdness Index. She said the bookstore itself rated a six-point-five, which was pretty high, but an actual ghost was worth at least two points.

The Beetle and Some Red Carnations

ON THE SATURDAY morning before Christmas, I watched through the viewing-room window as Charles Harkness left for his job at the bank. I was already wearing my jacket when he gently closed his front door, snuggled the collar of his long black overcoat around his neck, tightened his hat over his balding head, and strode toward downtown.

I wasn't the only one watching to make sure he was gone. The lace curtain in his parlor window was pulled back just a little, held by a tiny, wrinkled hand. I could picture his aunt Hetty's piercing, merry eyes and her smile-crinkled face.

As soon as Charles passed the big Christmas tree outside the Stone Church, I raced across the street and into their house.

"Why, here's Milly!" exclaimed Hetty when I got to

the parlor, just as if she hadn't stopped me the afternoon before when I delivered the newspaper and asked me to arrive at that exact moment. She had confided, "We need your help with a little surprise for Charles."

Hetty, stooped and shuffling, slowly pushed Martha in her wheelchair toward the dining room and motioned for me to follow.

"Are you sure we're doing the right thing?" Martha asked her sister. "We don't want Charles to think we're interfering."

"You're such a worrywart. Charles won't even know it was us.

"Thank you so much for coming, Milly dear," Hetty added in that sing-songy voice people save for five-year-olds. Maybe if you're ninety-two there's not much difference between five and eleven, so I didn't take it personally.

Yesterday's newspaper was carefully folded on the dining room table. Martha separated the sections and spread them out while Hetty got paper, scissors, and tape from the old sideboard.

"We need your help with some cutting and taping," Hetty said.

"And some delivering," added Martha.

That was when I realized I was about to participate in what Uncle Edgar had called The Quest.

Uncle Edgar knew about The Quest because Hetty and Martha had discussed their predicament last week when they had finally gotten around to planning their funerals. The aunts thought Charles was much too nice a man to be all alone in that big old house after they were gone—not that they planned on needing Uncle Edgar's services anytime soon. At sixty-two, Charles was still a young man, they said, but he was a little too shy. He'd never, all by himself, meet the woman of their dreams. Miss Annie MacPherson, a lively, outgoing, gray-haired lady who sang in the church choir, also served on the visiting committee. She had called on Hetty and Martha several times since the sisters stopped going to church because they were getting frail. They had both fallen in love with Annie, on Charles's behalf.

Right after Christmas, she was moving to another town and would be going to a different church. Charles would never meet her unless they did something and did it soon.

In Phase One of The Quest, the sisters had specifically invited Miss MacPherson to visit one afternoon around the time Charles usually arrived home from work. But it was the one day all year that he was late: The bank examiners were there.

In Phase Two, Hetty had convinced Charles to take her to church, even though she could barely walk and she hated to leave Martha home alone. She was hoping for a chance meeting. But Annie MacPherson was home sick that day.

Phase Three was their last chance. Soon Annie MacPherson would be lost to them—that is, to Charles—forever.

It seemed that the success of Phase Three was up to me.

"We need your help," Hetty was explaining, "because Martha can't see well enough up close and my hands are too shaky to cut straight." My assignment was to scan the headlines and the Christmas ads, cut out words and letters, and tape them on a piece of paper according to the sisters' instructions.

After a while, we had patched together a letter like the ransom notes you see in the movies.

> Dear Mr. Harkness,
> I have often seen you at church and think you look like a nice person. I am a lady about your age and would like to get to know you. Would you consider meeting me outside by the Christmas tree?
>
> A Secret Admirer

"What do you think, Milly?" Hetty asked. "You can give this to Charles after the Christmas Eve service. We'll do another note from Charles that you can give to Annie MacPherson. And the two of them will meet."

"I don't know. It might work. But there'll be lots of people at church on Christmas Eve. How will he know who she is?"

Then I remembered the beetle. "I know! The last two Sundays that I saw Annie MacPherson, she was wearing a big emerald pin shaped like a beetle on her winter coat. She must have bought it at the fall flea market. Why don't we say that?"

So we added a sentence to the note that was going to Charles: "I am wearing a big emerald pin shaped like a beetle." It took a while to piece the words together: In the middle of winter, nobody writes about beetles in the newspaper.

Then we patched another note together.

> Dear Miss MacPherson,
> I have often admired your singing. I'm a gentleman about your age and would like to get to know you. Would you consider meeting me outside by the Christmas tree?
>
> A Secret Admirer

Martha asked, "Shouldn't we add something so she'll know how to find him? Something like the beetle pin?"

Hetty laughed. "We can hardly expect Charles to wear a pin!"

"How about a flower?" I suggested. "Would he ever wear a flower in the buttonhole of his coat?"

"I think we could get him to do that," Hetty said.

So we added a sentence to the note that was going to Annie: "I am wearing a red carnation."

Once Hetty and Martha were satisfied with the notes, I solemnly promised to deliver them to Annie and Charles at the end of the Christmas Eve service. I also promised not to tell a soul about our plan.

Hetty reminded me that Uncle Edgar and I were invited to their house after the service for cocoa.

Then the sisters had nothing left to do but make

sure that their telescope was properly adjusted to focus on the Christmas tree outside the Stone Church on the corner. I had one more task, though.

I went to Flora's. "Hetty wants you to send a flower arrangement for Martha," I told Flora. "She wants some Christmas flowers, and she specifically asks you to be absolutely positively sure that you include some red carnations. She said to tell you that Martha especially likes red carnations."

Flora eyed me suspiciously. "What are those two rascals up to now?"

"I can't tell."

The first thing I did when we got to church on Christmas Eve was make sure Charles Harkness was wearing his flower. There he sat, a little behind us, with a red carnation in his buttonhole. I breathed a sigh of relief and relaxed.

I gazed casually around at the other church-goers. Suddenly I realized, to my absolute horror, that everyone else was wearing a red carnation, too! I looked in the choir loft. There was Annie MacPherson, right where she was supposed to be—wearing a red carnation pinned to her choir robe! In the pew next to us, Dim and Dimmer Downey wore twin red carnations. And here came Flora, with a basket of red carnations, giving one to everybody who didn't already have one.

Why did Flora have to choose this particular

Christmas to display the spirit of giving and donate her leftover red carnations to the church?

What was I going to do?

Of course, I could just do nothing. Maybe Charles and Annie would meet anyway.

Or maybe they wouldn't.

Pastor Paul preached in his deep, booming voice about the Christ child. This one small event, the birth of one little baby, he said, changed the entire course of human history.

I decided I'd better not leave Charles and Annie to chance. I should try to change the course of this particular human history myself.

But what should I do?

All through harking the herald angels and the little kids stumbling in their shepherd robes and the joys to the world, I was trying to figure it out.

We sang "Angels We Have Heard on High." When we got to the chorus, where everybody sings what the angels sang—"Glooooooooooooooooria"—I thought, That's who I need: Aunt Gloria here telling me what to do! But I wasn't hearing any of her helpful advice. I couldn't think of one thing Aunt Gloria had ever said that would help me in this situation.

No help from Aunt Gloria, none from Uncle Edgar or from Blane or Josie or Flora. This time, I had to figure things out all by myself.

Pastor Paul read the Christmas story in dramatic tones. The angels appeared to the shepherds and they were afraid. And the angels said to them, "Fear not: for, behold, I bring you tidings of great joy. . . ." When he got to the "not," he boomed extra loud.

Joyabounding, I realized, that's it! *Not*! That's all I need. A *not*! If everybody's wearing a red carnation, the man Annie should meet is the man who's *not*!

I knew where to find a not.

When everybody stood up to sing the last hymn, I begged Uncle Edgar, whispering as fast as I could, "Would you please do me a huge gigantic favor and I'll explain later? When the service is over, would you think of something to talk to Charles Harkness about, and don't let him leave the church until I get back?"

Uncle Edgar looked puzzled, but he said okay, and I hurried out the door at the front of the sanctuary. I ran down the stairs and out the side door.

It was a good thing that Grandma lived right next to the church. Grandma was away that day, but I knew where she kept the key. And of course I knew where yesterday's newspaper was because I had delivered it myself and left it on the kitchen table.

There are always lots of nots in the paper. I found one, got the scissors and tape from Grandma's kitchen drawer, and taped the not to the note that was going to Annie. Now the note said, "I am NOT wearing a red carnation." The note looked kind of funny, but I figured Annie would get the point.

I locked Grandma's house and flew in the side door of the church and down the stairs to the choir room.

The choir members were chatting and drinking coffee. I asked the first choir member I saw, "Would you please give this note to Annie MacPherson?" I was very careful to hand him the right note.

Then I dashed upstairs and into the sanctuary. Good old Uncle Edgar was talking a blue streak to Charles Harkness, who was too polite to interrupt. Most people had already filed out of the church. I paused to catch my breath and look calm.

"Excuse me," I said to Charles, "someone asked me to give you this note."

He gave me an inquiring look, slowly unfolded the note, and read it.

Then he smiled a little to himself and shook his head. "That someone wouldn't happen to be a pair of scheming little old ladies, would it?" he asked, showing the note to Uncle Edgar.

"I can't tell."

"I guess I'd better go see what this is all about," he said.

I stopped him. "Would you mind an awful lot if I asked if I could have your carnation? I'm . . . uh . . . making a collection."

"Sure," he said. He took it out of his buttonhole and handed it to me. Then he went out the front door. Uncle Edgar and I followed, in full view of anyone who happened to be watching the church through a telescope.

I went alone to visit Hetty and Martha after church. That was the Christmas Eve that old Mr. Young decided to go meet his maker and Uncle Edgar had to make the travel arrangements.

Thanks to the telescope, the sisters knew that Charles and Annie had met at the Christmas tree and walked away together. Of course, they didn't know what happened next. They speculated like two excited little girls trying to guess what might be in their Christmas stockings.

We were all in the parlor, drinking our second cups of cocoa, and the aunts were trying to remain calm, when Charles came in. He settled himself on the fluffy couch and I took him some cocoa. Then he said casually to the aunts, "I met an interesting person at church tonight."

"How nice," said Hetty blandly. "Who is it?"

"Her name is Annie MacPherson. She says she knows you two."

"Gracious, how would she know us?" asked Martha.

"She says she's been here to visit you."

Hetty seemed to think for a moment. "I bet I know who she is, Martha. She must be that tall woman, the one with the mustache, who told us about driving her truck to Alabama. Remember? We thought she might be a man in disguise."

I did everything I could to keep from smiling. I concentrated intently on my cocoa. I studied the marshmallows. I noticed that some weren't melting evenly. I rolled each marshmallow around with my spoon to coat it with chocolate. I poked the cocoa bubbles to break them.

"No," Martha was saying reflectively, "I believe Annie MacPherson was that pretty one with the curly gray hair. She'd be about your age, Charles. The one we thought was so friendly and had such a pleasant voice."

Charles said, "That's the one. Very pretty. Very pleasant. She sings in the choir. But there's something really odd." He sounded puzzled. "Miss MacPherson said that she received an anonymous letter—all taped together from words cut out of a newspaper, like a ransom note—signed by 'a secret admirer.' The letter asked her to meet this admirer at the Christmas tree after the service."

"My, that is odd," said Hetty.

"And what makes it even odder," Charles continued, "is that I received a note very much like hers, which is why I was at the Christmas tree to meet her."

"Good heavens," said Martha.

"I can't imagine who would do anything so strange. Can you?" asked Charles.

"A person would have to be very peculiar to think up something like that," Hetty agreed.

"Anyway," Charles said, "we chatted at the coffee shop for a while after the service. I like her. I asked her to come for lunch on New Year's Day. Is that all right with you ladies?"

I peeked at the aunts out of the corner of my eye. They were trying very hard not to look like the cats that swallowed the canary.

Hetty shrugged. "I guess that would be okay."

"It might be nice," Martha agreed.

"Maybe Milly and Edgar would like to come, too," Charles said with a tiny conspiratorial glance in my direction.

Then he turned to look at me fully. "And how is that carnation collection of yours coming along?"

"It's all coming along very well, thank you."

Stopping by the Woods

IN ENGLISH CLASS one February day, Josie passed me a note: "Groan. 4.5." It wasn't about the assignment. It was about the person we had to work with.

Our project was to illustrate a poem. Mr. French said we should try to "capture the spirit" of the poem. He told us we could work in teams of two or three, so naturally Josie and I wanted to work together. But Carol Jones's best friend, Ashley, was on a ski trip in Colorado and Carol didn't have a partner. Guess whose team he made her join. Carol was as happy about this as we were.

This was our poem.

"Stopping by Woods on a Snowy Evening"
by Robert Frost

Whose woods these are I think I know,
His house is in the village, though;
He will not see me stopping here
To watch his woods fill up with snow.

My little horse must think it queer
To stop without a farmhouse near
Between the woods and frozen lake
The darkest evening of the year.

He gives his harness bells a shake
To ask if there is some mistake.
The only other sound's the sweep
Of easy wind and downy flake.

The woods are lovely, dark, and deep,
But I have promises to keep,
And miles to go before I sleep,
And miles to go before I sleep.

Carol, Josie, and I met to plan how we would illustrate the poem.

"I'm glad we got this one," I said. "Sometimes I feel like that person in the poem, don't you? Like when you're with lots of people you don't know, and you wish you could be quiet and by yourself and read or think about things?"

"It's a little too peaceful for me," Josie said, "but I know what you mean."

"This is boring," Carol complained. "Why don't we just draw a picture and get it over with?"

"Probably everybody will do that," said Josie. "It would be more fun to do something different and surprise everybody. Maybe we could do a skit."

"How about a video?" I suggested. "It would be like making a movie. We could act the poem out on tape.

Then we could read it while people watch the tape. It would be live and taped, too. Multimedia."

Josie said, "Great idea! I'm sure my dad would let me use his video camera. But if we do a skit, we'll need a horse costume. Where would we get a horse costume?"

"Maybe the high school drama department has one," I said. Then, "Wait a second! Joyabounding! Why do we need a costume when we could use a real horse!"

We both looked at Carol. "I don't know if I feel like lending Blazing Champion to people who don't know anything about horses just so they can make a video."

"It's your project, too," Josie reminded her.

"But he's never been taped before. He might get nervous and scared."

"But you know all about horses," I said. "You could help him relax. Besides, if we made a video you could star in it. There's only one person in the poem, and that person has to know how to drive a horse. That would be you. Josie can run the camera. I'll be the director. And you can be the star."

When she heard the word *star*, Carol perked up.

"I wouldn't have to dress like a man, would I?" she asked.

We studied the poem. Nowhere did it say that the "I" in the poem was a man.

"Then I could get my hair done"—she was thinking out loud—"and wear my new coat with the fur collar."

"We'll need a wagon, too, or a sleigh or something," Josie said.

"I think the equestrian center has a little cart. We could probably use that."

For a place to film, we'd need woods and a road where we could work away from the traffic. Bentwood didn't have a lake, so we'd have to do without that.

"I know the perfect place!" I said. "Zeena Fovia's driveway. It's like a long road, and it's woodsy. We have to shoot in the dark, because that's what it says in the poem. But Zeena has all her lights on at night. That will give us some light to shoot by."

"Did you say Zeena Fovia?" asked Carol. "Weird Zeena?"

"Do you know Zeena?"

"Sure. Until I was about five she lived right next door to us. Then she went crazy and sold everything and bought that ugly little house. How do you know Zeena?"

"She's a friend of ours," I said firmly. I didn't want to hear any more about "weird" Zeena. Then I thought how strange that was: Josie rated Zeena high on the Weirdness Index, and I didn't mind at all. Maybe that was because Josie knew Zeena as well as I did and liked her as much as I did. When Carol said "weird," it sounded different. Carol hardly knew Zeena. She hadn't seen her in years. How could *she* decide whether Zeena was weird or not?

"If I can get Zeena's permission," I said to Carol, "would your father bring your horse and the cart over to Zeena's?"

"My father's way too busy. But he pays the equestrian center a lot of money to take care of Blazing Champion. Somebody there can take them over and get them when we're through."

Zeena was thrilled that we wanted to use her driveway. We scheduled the shoot for early Saturday evening, because it was supposed to snow a little then.

On Friday, Josie said to me, "I think I should see the horse ahead of time to help me plan the shoot."

No kids we knew except Ashley had ever seen Blazing Champion, but we had heard lots of stories about his prize-winning wonderfulness.

Josie and I went to the equestrian center after school. We looked around the corral. No horse. Just a tired-looking gray pony about the size of a big dog.

We asked a man at the stable, "Where's Carol Jones's horse?"

"Right over there." He pointed to the pony.

Josie and I looked at each other in disbelief. She said, "That's Blazing Champion the wonder steed that we've heard so much about?"

We walked to the fence for a closer look. He didn't move. He blinked at us sleepily.

Josie said, "I think Blazing Champion's fire went out a long time ago. No wonder Carol didn't want us to use him in the video."

"In the poem, the horse is little," I said, remembering. "But I didn't picture him *this* little."

"I can shoot him from down low. That'll make him look bigger."

"It's a good thing you're a genius," I said.

On Saturday morning, I got a panicky call from Carol.

"I can't do it, Milly! I can't be in the video!"

"Why? What's the matter?"

"I have a zit!"

"What?"

"I have a great big ugly pimple. Right on the end of my nose!"

"Couldn't you put some pimple gunk on it? No one will notice."

"Yes, they will! It's huge! I can't be on video with a big zit on my nose. Everybody will laugh at me."

"No, they won't. Lots of people get zits. It's not your fault."

"Anyway, I'm not doing it."

"But we can't quit now. It's too late to start another project."

"You'll just have to shoot it without me."

"But it's your horse. We can't shoot it without the horse. And we can't have the horse without you because Josie and I don't know anything about horses. Besides," I added, "if you're not there, you won't get any credit for the project and maybe you won't pass the course."

Silence.

"I didn't think about that. My father would kill me if

I failed English. Okay, I'll come, and I'll help with Blazing Champion, but I won't be in the video."

"So who's going to be the star?" I hoped the word *star* might change her mind again.

"I don't want to be the star if I can't look perfect. You'll have to do it yourself."

"Me! I can't act! I'm the director!"

"You'll just have to do it."

I wondered if Carol was afraid that if she appeared on the video, everyone would guess that the tired little pony was Blazing Champion.

"By the way," I said, "Josie's planning to shoot Blazing Champion from down low. He'll look really really big."

More silence.

"I'm not being in the video," she insisted, and hung up.

I phoned Josie.

"I don't want to be the star," I protested. "I'd be too embarrassed."

"You don't have any choice. I have to run the camera. Besides, I bet you'll be great. You might even like it."

When we gathered at Zeena's for the shoot, Carol wasn't wearing her new coat with the fur collar. She *was* wearing a giant zit on her nose and a grumpy frown on the rest of her face, but Josie and I pretended not to notice her nose or her disposition. It was snowing very gently, a few leisurely, fat, fluffy flakes.

By the time Carol and the equestrian-center man hitched Blazing Champion to the two-wheeled pony cart at the bottom of the long, narrow driveway, the lights were coming on in Zeena's house.

Our plan was for Josie to tape me as I drove the cart slowly halfway up the driveway, stopped and looked around to watch the woods fill up with snow, told the little horse to "giddup," and drove to the top of the driveway.

I climbed into the pony cart, feeling very insecure and even stranger than when I rode on Grandma's motorcycle. At least on the motorcycle I was with someone who knew how to drive. And nobody was taking my picture.

Fortunately, Blazing Champion was standing very still. In fact, he had dozed off.

"Before you start the camera, I better practice making him go," I called to Josie. "What do I do, Carol?"

Carol handed me the reins.

"Just jiggle the rains and say 'giddup,' " she said.

I jiggled. "Giddup," I said.

Nothing.

"Harder," she said.

I jiggled harder. "Giddup," I said louder.

This time he turned his head, opened one eye, and glared at me like I was annoying him.

"Say it like you mean it," Carol said impatiently.

"Giddup!" I yelled, and whapped him on the back with the reins.

Blazing Champion suddenly jerked forward and bolted up the driveway. I flew by Josie, screaming to Carol, "How do I make him stop?"

Carol ran up beside me and grabbed the bridle. "Whoa," she said firmly, and he stopped. "Back," she ordered, and he began to back down to the foot of the driveway.

"This is definitely not working, Josie," I said as we backed past her.

"Yes, it is. You look great!"

"Well, I can't drive the horse. We better think of something else."

Carol said she could lead Blazing Champion on my left. Then Josie could shoot on my right, aiming the camera so Carol wouldn't show in the picture.

"Okay, go!" Josie called when the camera was ready. Carol said, "Giddup," and Blazing Champion and I proceeded slowly up the driveway. When we got to Josie, we stopped. Josie brought the camera close to my face. I felt very self-conscious, but I looked around at the woods as thoughtfully as I could. Josie moved the camera away from my face, to Blazing Champion, to the woods. She turned it off.

"Good acting," she told me.

"Really?"

"Directors don't lie about good acting."

Just then Zeena scurried out of the house carrying a little paper bag. She was so happy to see that we were right on schedule with our project, she said, and she hoped it was going well, and it was very nice to see our friend Carol again after all these years, and didn't I look wonderful in the cart, and how nice of the people at the equestrian center to bring the horse and cart over, and she was glad she was able to help by lending us her driveway and she hoped there was enough light, and would we like a warm chocolate chip cookie just out of the oven.

Of course, we said yes to the cookies and we each took one out of the bag.

"Where are the harness bells?" asked Josie through a mouthful of cookie. "Carol, did you bring any harness bells?"

"Harness bells? Nobody told me I was supposed to bring harness bells."

"It says it in the poem."

"I guess I didn't notice."

Zeena sprang into action. "I don't know anything about horses," she said, "but I got some lovely jingle bells from a mail order catalog to put on my front door at Christmastime. The catalog house was very busy, of course, and they never got around to sending me the bells, and I didn't get them until after Christmas, so they're brand new, but I kept them anyway because, you know, there'll always be another Christmas, and I think they'll be perfect and I'll just go get them."

As Zeena rushed into the house, Carol said, "She's even crazier than I remembered."

"She's very nice," I said, and Josie added pointedly, "We're lucky she's helping us with the harness bells."

We tied Zeena's front-door jingle bells to Blazing Champion's harness.

"Okay," Josie said. "How do we make him give the harness bells a shake?"

Blazing Champion was blinking sleepily. He wasn't in a shaking mood.

"I don't know any command for shake," Carol said.

As we tried to figure out what to do, Zeena began to stroke Blazing Champion's nose. She told him what a pretty pony he was, and what a talented actor, and didn't he enjoy being in a movie, and it was too bad his first acting job was in the snow. She took a cookie out of her bag and offered it to him.

He munched. Then he threw back his head and whinnied, shaking from his nose to his tail. The bells jingled.

"Do that again!" Josie said as she turned the camera on. So Zeena gave Blazing Champion another cookie. He munched, whinnied, and shook again. The shot was done. Blazing Champion went back to sleep.

Suddenly there was a second of absolute silence—one of those surprising still moments that can happen right in the middle of everybody being busy and noisy. I could hear the pat of fluffy snowflakes when they landed softly on my sleeve. A breeze rustled lightly through the bare trees. I looked into the woods. Zeena's woods really *were* "lovely, dark, and deep."

I whispered, "Look! Listen! It's just like in the poem." None of us moved or spoke in the sharp night air. Not even Zeena. Just like the person in the poem, I didn't want that peaceful moment to end.

But we had to finish our tape.

By now, I was more comfortable with the camera pointing at me. I was feeling the spirit of the poem. I cocked my head to listen to the breeze. I gazed at the snow. I was an actor.

"Very good," Josie said.

We needed one last shot. Josie would tape the cart from behind as we continued up the driveway.

I held the reins. Carol held the bridle. I pretended to tell Blazing Champion to giddup.

"Giddup," Carol said. He woke up, but he didn't move.

She yanked. "Giddup," she said, a little louder.

Nothing.

She pulled. *"Giddup!"* she shouted at the top of her lungs.

More nothing. It was past Blazing Champion's bedtime. Carol stomped off. She plunked herself on the edge of Zeena's porch. "Darn horse," she grumbled.

Josie turned the camera off. She muttered, "It's a good thing Carol's here to keep him from getting too nervous and scared."

Zeena began to pat Blazing Champion's nose again and croon. "He's such a good actor, but he's just a little sleepy, that's all, and maybe if he could wake up just a teeny bit he'd like another cookie." She opened the cookie bag and held it under his nose. Blazing Champion's head jerked up.

He followed the cookie bag all the way up to the porch while Josie shot.

"That's a wrap!" Josie called.

"Does that mean you're finished? Come on in the house, then," Zeena said, feeding Blazing Champion one last cookie. "We can look at your video and see what you've got."

While Carol phoned the equestrian center to come for her and Blazing Champion, Josie and I wrote the credits and taped them:

"Stopping by Woods on a Snowy Evening"
Written by Robert Frost
Starring Millicent Moore
Produced and Directed by Josephine Martinez
Horse Handler: Carol Jones
Technical Consultant and Caterer: Zeena Fovia
No animals were harmed in the filming of this video.

Then Zeena cleared a pile of catalogs away from the VCR and we all sat down on the floor to watch.

I had never seen myself on tape. I really looked thoughtful when I was supposed to be thoughtful and sleepy when I was supposed to be sleepy.

"You all did a wonderful job, and Milly, you look just lovely," Zeena said.

"You did great," Josie agreed.

"You should have worn some makeup," Carol said.

I grinned at Josie and she grinned back.

After Carol and Blazing Champion left with the equestrian-center man, Zeena told us she so much enjoyed helping, and it was wonderful that Carol had a chance to work with two such nice girls and wasn't it too bad about Carol, being so beautiful and so rich but so grumpy, but Carol had always been like that, nothing was ever good enough, nothing made her happy, she was just born crabby and she was teaching that darling little pony to be crabby, too, and Zeena had always felt sorry for poor Carol Jones.

We got an A on our project. Mr. French was so proud of our video that he showed it to everyone in the school, over and over, and we had to take turns reading the poem.

The kids joked that I was a movie star and pretended they wanted my autograph. I had never been the star of anything. It was embarrassing at first, but I liked when people said I had done a good job. After a while I had to admit to Josie that acting on camera wasn't so bad once I got used to it, and that being a star could be fun.

Josie said we should always remember to be thankful for zits.

Josie took some points off Carol's Weirdness Index. We decided it wasn't her fault that she was born crabby. And we never told anyone that the sleepy gray pony on our video was Carol's Blazing Champion.

Good-bye Again

I WAS SPRAWLED out on the porch swing, reading, on a warm April afternoon. Aunt Gloria had died almost a year before. I hadn't received any "helpful advice" for several months.

Suddenly, I heard her voice. Plain as day.

"Sit up straight and pay attention."

I bolted upright.

"Tell your uncle Edgar to forget my memorial service. Tell him to just do my viewing again."

I found Uncle Edgar hunched over the kitchen table, planning the service that would honor Aunt Gloria's memory. I didn't like to disturb him while he was concentrating. I slid into the chair across from him as quietly as I could.

"Excuse me, Uncle Edgar, can I talk to you for a minute?"

Uncle Edgar knew I wouldn't interrupt him unless it

was important. He peered at me over his reading glasses. He focused on me gradually, as if his brain had been a long way away and had just barely caught the bus back.

"What's the matter, Milly?"

"It's Aunt Gloria. I hear her talking to me."

He looked concerned. "How long has this been going on?"

"I heard her a lot right after she died, but not lately. Until today."

"Why didn't you tell me? And what happened today?"

"I didn't tell you before because she was always just giving me some of her helpful advice. But today she told me something to say to you."

"What was that?"

"She says not to have a memorial service. She says we have to do her viewing again."

He looked off into the distance for a few seconds. I thought his shoulders sagged a little.

"Did she say what was wrong with the first one?" He had tried so hard to make it perfect.

"No."

"Keep listening. She probably will."

Aunt Gloria's voice found me again later that afternoon as I did homework in my room.

"Tell your uncle Edgar no carnations. I hate carnations. They smell like a funeral parlor. He played that awful tape, the one with the organ music. I would rather have a symphony. And he shouldn't have played that 'Amazing Grace' record. It got Angus MacDonald to bawling and disrupting everything."

Aunt Gloria didn't say anything about the dress we picked, so I figured at least we did *that* right. I didn't remember Angus MacDonald bawling that much, but he probably did.

Uncle Edgar was in the embalming room, working on old Mrs. Johnson, who had died in her sleep early that morning. He was putting makeup on her so everybody could say how good and healthy she looked.

"Excuse me, Uncle Edgar," I said. "It's Aunt Gloria again."

"Did she say what she wants?"

"She didn't like the music and the flowers." I asked him, "Do we really have to do the viewing again?"

"Her spirit probably won't be able to move on and be at peace until we do. I hate to think of Gloria not being at peace. We'll try to make things just the way she wants them."

He added, "Tomorrow, after we finish with Mrs. Johnson, we'll do your aunt Gloria again."

Uncle Edgar knew a lot about dead people, one thing being that maybe they don't see everything too clearly, since they're in a place where the atmosphere might be a little foggy. So if you're doing something for them, you don't have to be too careful about the details. At least that's what we were hoping. Because doing the viewing again presented a few real challenges.

The main challenge was that the Commonwealth of Massachusetts strongly prefers that once a person is buried, they should stay buried. That meant we had to find a stand-in (maybe you'd call it a lie-in) for Aunt Gloria. Since Uncle Edgar didn't want anyone else to know what we were doing, there was nobody we could use but me.

The second main challenge was the flowers. Somehow we had to arrange flowers all around the room that were not carnations. We couldn't order flowers from Flora, which everybody always did for viewings. Flora knew what was happening to people in Bentwood before they knew it themselves. She would definitely ask some serious questions if we ordered flowers and she didn't know of any newly dead person.

That's why we will always be grateful to Mrs. Johnson. On the day of her funeral, after the last mourner left the cemetery, Uncle Edgar loaded the floral tributes in the hearse. When he got home, we carefully picked all the carnations out of the tributes, and I made notes about which ones came from which arrangements. Then we placed the carnationless tributes all around the viewing room.

Fortunately, Uncle Edgar had a casket in the showroom that looked a lot like Aunt Gloria's. He put that on the casket stand.

The next big challenge was the mourners. Naturally, we couldn't invite everybody who had been there the first time.

Joyabounding, that's when I had my most brilliant and creative idea.

I climbed up to the attic and brought down my boxes of dolls and stuffed animals that Aunt Gloria had put away when she decided it was time for me to grow up and be a lady.

The chairs were still in place for Mrs. Johnson's viewing. I carefully arranged the dolls and animals, one on each chair. Of course, Uncle Edgar had been at the first viewing, so he could be himself. The Madeline doll sat in my chair. Raggedy Ann made a good Flora because of the wild red hair. I had a Howdy Doody marionette someone gave Uncle Edgar when he was little: Howdy made a good Angus MacDonald because he was skinny and had freckles. I didn't have a doll like Charles Harkness, so I put a plump Winnie-the-Pooh in his chair.

I chose a little teddy bear for my grandmother, not because anyone would ever mistake Grandma for a teddy bear, but because she had sent me that one when I was a baby. The Ken doll was an obvious choice for Blane. Barbie would do for Carol Jones's mother.

One by one, I filled the chairs. The guests sat as quiet and solemn as any mourners I have ever seen at a viewing.

Then I went to my room and put on the frilly pink dress I wore at the first viewing, like the one Aunt

Gloria had worn herself. I figured that with the postlife fog factor we were counting on, maybe Aunt Gloria wouldn't notice the pin holes from the Christmas tinsel we'd pinned on for Josie's Halloween costume.

I was nervous about the next part. Like most people, I had never been in a casket. But I told myself that all I had to do was act dead. If this was like being in a play, I didn't even have to memorize any lines. And nobody was taping me.

"Are you sure you want to do this?" Uncle Edgar asked me gently when I returned to the viewing room.

I thought about Aunt Gloria, how she wasn't able to move on and be at peace. I wondered if she had ever really been at peace in all her life. I remembered what Grandma said, that Aunt Gloria had been fond of me and wanted me to be just like her. I thought about all of Aunt Gloria's "advice" and I knew that, in her own way, she had been trying her best to help me grow up. I hadn't heard any advice lately. Maybe that meant I was doing okay on my own now.

So I took a deep breath and said, "I want to do it."

Uncle Edgar helped me climb into the casket. I lay there with my eyes closed and my hands clasped at my waist, very quiet and still.

I stayed motionless while Uncle Edgar played his new tape, *The World's Greatest Symphonic Hits*. He did not play the "Amazing Grace" tape, though I was pretty sure that, this time, Mr. Angus "Howdy" MacDonald would not have bawled too much.

After the music was over, Uncle Edgar helped me out and closed the casket. "Good job," he whispered, hugging me.

Instead of saying good-bye to the mourners and returning them to the attic, I carried them to my room and arranged them on the bookshelves next to my books. Maybe I wouldn't play with them much anymore, but I could at least enjoy their company.

Early the next morning, before anyone else in Bentwood was up, Uncle Edgar and I replaced the carnations in their proper floral tributes and he took them back to Mrs. Johnson at the cemetery.

I never heard another word from Aunt Gloria. Either the fog held, or we had done everything right.

One Ordinary Day

IT WAS MAY, and everybody in school was entering the Annual Ordinary Day Parade Essay Contest. We all wanted to win. The winner would be grand marshall and lead the parade.

Bentwood's Ordinary Day Parade was on an unspecial day, a Wednesday or Thursday. Everybody took the afternoon off, and we spent it doing ordinary things. Anyone could march in the parade. You could wear whatever you wanted; most people wore their everyday clothes. The high school band played the usual marches, like "Stars and Stripes Forever." We all paraded from the town hall to the middle school gym, where we played games everybody knew and ate ordinary food like hot dogs and popcorn, and vanilla, chocolate, or strawberry ice cream.

The grand marshall stood on a stage and read his or

her winning essay about what it means to be an ordinary person.

One afternoon I was delivering papers on my bike, daydreaming about being grand marshall. I wasn't watching where I was going, and as I crossed a side street I crashed right into Angus MacDonald's antique Studebaker.

The next thing I knew, I was waking up in a hospital bed. Uncle Edgar was holding one hand in both of his and looking worried. Grandma was stroking my other hand, looking concerned but confident. Angus MacDonald was standing at the foot of my bed, moaning, "Ah, the poor wee lassie, she ran right into me," with tears in his eyes.

Every part of my body was fighting to prove that it could hurt the most. The winner was my right leg, which was wrapped in a huge cast and hanging from a frame over the bed.

I felt that I should say something. In books, someone in my position usually says, "What happened?" But I remembered what happened. I just didn't feel like talking about it.

Dr. Sherwood strode in.

"Well, Milly, you finally woke up." He peered into my eyes, felt my pulse, and turned to Uncle Edgar. "The X rays show she doesn't have a concussion. I don't think there are any internal injuries. She doesn't look too good right now, because of the scrapes and bruises. But I don't see any serious injuries except for that leg. She smashed it up pretty well. She'll have to be in traction for a while."

"How long is a while?" Uncle Edgar asked anxiously.

"We'll have to see how she does."

Pretty soon my room looked like a greenhouse. Flora must have worked overtime filling orders from everybody I knew. My favorite was from Charles Harkness and his fiancée, Annie MacPherson: a vase of red carnations.

Uncle Edgar stayed with me every minute that he could. He asked the doctors and nurses so many questions, they probably wished somebody would die so he'd have something else to do.

Josie rushed in each afternoon. She was in charge of delivering schoolwork so I wouldn't get too far behind. She brought me a giant bag of M&Ms, then ate most of them herself.

A lot of other kids visited, too. Even Carol Jones. She only stayed long enough to ask how I was doing, but she left a get-well card with a huge gold star pasted on the envelope. The card was signed "Carol and Blazing Champion."

Blane talked the nurses into showing him my X rays.

Grandma gave me a book of mystery stories. "We can't let you be tempted to watch TV," she said, "or your brain will turn to Jell-O." Bob and Gracie Arnold brought me books from their store. Gracie brought *Favorite Poems of America's Youth*. Bob chose *You and Your Bones*.

When Angus MacDonald saw that Uncle Edgar had bought me a portable CD player, he gave me a CD of "Amazing Grace" sung twenty-five different ways.

Zeena Fovia sent me some large, purple fleece socks from L. L. Bean. "Once you can get up and around," she said when she called me one night, "your toes are going to be cold sticking out of that cast. I remember once, when I was young, I slipped on the ice in the dead of winter and broke my ankle and I had to wear a cast for weeks and my toes were so cold, I didn't think they'd ever be warm again for the rest of my life."

In the hospital I had plenty of time to think about my essay for the Ordinary Day Parade and what it means to be ordinary.

Aunt Gloria had said that Bentwood was full of peculiar people. Did that mean Aunt Gloria was an "ordinary" person? She surely thought other people should behave the way she did. But I didn't know one single person who reminded me of Aunt Gloria!

Josie rated people on her Weirdness Index. But sometimes I thought Josie was weird, and sometimes she thought I was, and she was my very best friend. In fact, we liked *all* the weird people we knew.

Lying in my hospital room, I was surrounded by presents from the peculiar and weird—and also very nice—people of Bentwood.

Maybe "peculiar" and "ordinary" depended on who was doing the describing. The people I knew probably thought they were ordinary themselves. When other people were different from them, the other people seemed peculiar. The more different they were, the more peculiar they seemed.

Aunt Gloria was right: Bentwood *was* full of peculiar people. It was also full of ordinary people. And they were all the same people.

So in my essay, I said that there's no such thing as an ordinary person. I didn't use Aunt Gloria's word, *peculiar*, of course. That would have been impolite. I used the word *extraordinary* because every peculiar and ordinary person I had come to know during the past year was special in some way.

Josie handed in my essay for me.

A couple of days later, Uncle Edgar had some good news and some bad news.

"Your essay won the Ordinary Day Parade Contest," he said, smiling at me both proudly and sadly, "but—"

"Yes!" I interrupted, waving my arms in the air. I was so excited I could have jumped all around the room, except I couldn't get out of bed because of the traction contraption.

Then I paused. "But what?"

"But I'm afraid Dr. Sherwood says you'll still be in traction the day of the parade."

"You mean I won't even be able to leave the hospital? They can't just give me a regular cast and let me do the parade in a wheelchair or something?"

"I'm afraid not," he said, taking my hand and sitting down next to the bed.

"There must be something we can do," I said.

We sat in silence together while we wondered what to do.

Suddenly I thought of Uncle Edgar's flower car. The shiny black car with the long, open back led funeral processions, carrying all the floral tributes to the cemetery. I looked around at the frame that held my leg suspended. Joyabounding!

"I bet this traction contraption would fit in the back of your flower car! Maybe I can be the grand marshall anyway!"

Uncle Edgar scrunched his eyebrows. He was thinking it over. He shook his head doubtfully.

"I'll talk to Dr. Sherwood," he said, "but don't get your hopes up."

In a while, he was back with a yardstick.

"Don't get excited," he said. "I'm just measuring."

The next time I saw him, he was wearing a huge grin.

"Dr. Sherwood says we can do it."

So on the day of the Ordinary Day Parade, the doctors and Uncle Edgar loaded me and the whole contraption into the back of the flower car.

I wore a bright yellow dress that Aunt Gloria had made for me. Josie picked it out. Even *I* could see that sometimes it's important to get dressed up. Flora decorated my cast with purple and yellow flowers. I wore Zeena's purple fleece sock over my cold toes.

And I led the parade in style, propped up on pillows, facing backward in the back of the flower car, a bright yellow blanket tucked around my lap and left leg, my right leg dangling above me. Uncle Edgar drove very slowly so as not to jiggle it. People along the route waved to me, and I waved back. Josie taped me and the whole parade.

Uncle Edgar drove the flower car into the gym through the delivery doors. He stood beside the car while the mayor introduced me as the little girl with the big leg. The mayor gave me the microphone and I read my essay, speaking as firmly and clearly as I could from my reclining position.

Everyone applauded. Kids cheered. Grown-ups came to shake my hand. Josie brought me a huge dish of chocolate ice cream.

Uncle Edgar was beaming. I motioned for him to come closer. I said, "I bet this is the most fun you ever had with the flower car."

"It sure is." He laughed.

Josie told me, "Thanks to your brilliant and creative idea, I can score this Ordinary Day a perfect ten on the Weirdness Index—the first perfect ten in the history of the Index."

"Joyabounding," we said together. Josie grinned and helped herself to a giant spoonful of my ice cream.